Caroline b Cooney

Driver's Ed

mammoth

First published in the USA 1994
by Bantam Doubleday Dell Books for Young Readers
a division of Bantam Doubleday Dell Publishing Group, Inc
First published in Great Britain 1997
by Mammoth, an imprint of Reed International Books Ltd
Michelin House, 81 Fulham Road, London SW3 6RB
and Auckland, Melbourne, Singapore and Toronto

ISBN 0 7497 2600 8

10 9 8 7 6 5 4 3 2 1

A CIP catalogue record for this title
is available from the British Library

Printed and bound in Great Britain
by Cox & Wyman Ltd, Reading, Berkshire

19684
FICTION

for friends
especially Lynne and Harold
and music teachers
especially Tahme

CHAPTER 1

Remy Marland crossed her fingers and prayed to the God of Driver's Education that she would get to drive today. Remy's fingers were splayed on the denim of her torn, pale blue jeans, inches from the second most desirable piece of laminated paper on earth. (The first, of course, was her future driver's license.)

Next to her, Christine prayed not to drive today or ever. Poor Christine held her shiny name tag in her lap, ready for Remy to snatch up.

"All right, class," said Mr. Fielding. He didn't look at them, because he never looked at them. He looked only at his enrollment book. "Remy, Christine, and Morgan will drive with me today."

"Yes!" yelled Remy. She didn't have to exchange a name tag after all. She jumped up so fast, she knocked her books on the floor, tried to grab them, and tripped over Taft's extended legs.

This was not clumsiness. It was calculated. Remy was the Distraction Princess, because even Mr. Fielding might one day catch on to what was happening.

"I love driii-ving," sang Remy. She had a beautiful voice, and enough poise to sing her way through all her

1

classes. The class smiled indulgently at her, the way you smile at a favorite pet.

Christine lay low. Many hands stretched out to grab Christine's name tag so they could go driving in her place, but Lark, of course, got there first. Lark was small, almost a shadow of the other girls in the class, but her shadow was invariably at the front of the line.

"Taft," said Mr. Fielding, "you and Chase show the class this film on drug and alcohol abuse. Everybody behave. Mrs. Bee will be watching."

With a huge melodramatic gesture Mrs. Bee, their elegant librarian, threw sunglasses on the bridge of her nose to let Mr. Fielding see that no, she would not be watching.

Driver's Ed was assigned to a glass-walled cubicle off the library, making the unfortunate librarian responsible for supervising the kids not going driving. Mrs. Bee pointed out that if this were a sport, the coach would get extra money for handling an extra group. Librarians never got extra money for anything, so Mrs. Bee wore her sunglasses and supervised nothing.

The class had given her earplugs as well, which Mrs. Bee was perfectly willing to wave in Mr. Fielding's face (or the principal's, should he come by), but she said they felt icky, and just to close the glass door for auditory privacy. Auditory privacy was almost always needed.

Remy bundled Mr. Fielding through the library. She had to set the pace or half the period would be wasted just approaching the Driver's Ed car.

Remy gave a circular wave to the left-behinds. "Now, children," she called back. "No gossip. No sick cartoons drawn on the blackboard. No carving of four-letter words into somebody's crew cut."

Jealous would-be drivers snarled and then laughed. Remy got more turns at driving than anybody, and most of the time it was okay. The boys—since they were boys and therefore thick—did not know why Remy was always getting other people's turns. The girls —since they were girls and grade-A schemers—understood perfectly.

Remy Marland was in love with Morgan.

Morgan, however, didn't know she existed. Since true love is a beautiful thing that requires two participants, the girls didn't mind switching so Remy could have extra turns in the backseat with Morgan.

Remy admired Morgan from the rear. From all angles Morgan Campbell was worthy of adoration.

"You drive, Remy," said Mr. Fielding, checking her off on his clipboard.

Remy exulted. It would have been wonderful to sit in back with Morgan, but it was more wonderful to drive. She slid behind the wheel, surveying her instrument panel like a bomber pilot heading to the battlefield.

Remy did not know where she was going, but one thing for sure.

She was going to get there fast.

Driver's Ed was like so many things about school.

If the parents only knew . . .

Mr. Fielding would take three kids: two in the backseat observing while one drove; he himself the front passenger.

Off they'd go, straight onto the turnpike, at that

terrifying cloverleaf where both interstates merge. Mr. Fielding explained that since fear was a problem for new drivers, the first thing student drivers must do on the road was conquer fear.

He himself didn't even have interest, let alone fear. Mr. Fielding would listen to his Walkman. His favorite talk station specialized in money discussions. Now and then Mr. Fielding would tell everybody how to invest their pensions.

A fifteen- or sixteen-year-old who'd never before held a steering wheel in his two shaking hands had one hundred yards in which to accelerate to sixty-five miles per hour. Then, either there was a space between the trucks and cars whipping past on their way to distant states . . . or there wasn't.

Either the student merged . . . or he plowed along the shoulder, metal barriers sickeningly close to the right fenders and unforgiving traffic sickeningly close to the left fenders.

The two backseat drivers, sweaty with panic, would be sticking their fingers down the filthy seat cracks, trying to buckle their seat belts prior to collision. Once they realized Mr. Fielding was not going to get involved, they would scream hints of their own.

"Get in! Get in!"

"There's a space!"

"Quick! You're gonna kill us!"

The student driver would jerk the poor old battered Driver's Ed car into the correct lane.

Mr. Fielding would continue gazing out the right window instead of the left, watching the landscape and not the traffic.

Nobody had died yet, or even had an accident,

mainly because oncoming traffic didn't want to die or have an accident either.

Few people conquered fear on the first day of Driver's Ed. In fact, several members of the class developed so much *more* fear that they refused to go driving again.

"Have your parents taken you out in your new car yet?" Lark asked Remy.

Remy hated trying to talk while driving. There was far too much to think about. Traffic behind and ahead. Traffic to the left and traffic to the right. Curbs and signs and red lights and turns. Foot on brake and hands on wheel. Eyes on mirrors and ears on sirens.

And the Driver's Ed car was an automatic. She'd never be able to drive standard. What if she also had clutches and shifting and gears? "Uh. No," she said.

Remy Marland was the only person in the eleven A.M. Driver's Ed class who already owned a car. Her parents had assigned her the wonderful role of family chauffeur and errand runner. On the day she turned sixteen, she would become the taker of baby brother to day care and middle brother to orthodontist and karate.

"Actually," said Lark, "you will be the family slave. An unpaid, unappreciated beast of burden. Trapped around the clock in the very same car with Henry and Mac. A lifetime occupation of strapping the baby in and out of the car seat. Sentenced to hard labor, breathing the same air as Mac, the state Fart Master."

It was true that Remy did not even like to have her clothes washed in the same cycle as Mac's, lest she be contaminated.

Here he was in eighth grade—almost fourteen years

5

old—and Mac had yet to do any growing. He was the same size, height, and weight he'd been in sixth grade. Being eye level with girls' elbows made him hostile. His life's goal was to be a little more disgusting today than he had been yesterday.

Just last night he'd wrapped his used dental floss around Remy's toothbrush in case she'd forgotten they shared a bathroom.

However, as driver, Remy would have the upper hand. If Mac tried anything with her, she'd stop the car two miles from his karate lesson and see what he did then.

Of course, it was Mac. He'd probably hijack her.

But Remy visualized her license life as one of dropping Mac off—emptying the car of Mac, as opposed to being locked in with him. Mac's karate, tennis, swimming, and weight lifting were at different places, reached by different roads at different times of day. Remy would triumph, easily making tough turns against traffic, whipping into teeny little parallel parking spaces, brilliantly passing slow cars on narrow roads.

"You're just jealous," said Remy.

"Better believe it," said Lark. "Your own car? Of course you'll have to chauffeur me, too, you know, because I'm your friend."

Mr. Fielding heard nothing.

Not traffic.

Not blowing horns.

Not sirens.

And most of all, not student conversation.

Mr. Fielding was looking at the scenery his student driver passed—too fast—wishing he had a different life.

6

A life without kids with these ridiculous names.

What had happened to the solid names of old? Karen and Susan and Janet? Peter and Robert and Jim? Mr. Fielding's Driver's Education classes had boys with last names for first names: Taft, Chase, and Morgan. Girls with names from nowhere: Lark and Joss and Remy.

It seemed to Mr. Fielding that these were interchangeable names. These kids had no personalities and could have been anyone at all. Their names never stuck to them the way real names would, but were just sounds. Syllables. Signifying nothing.

These kids, like their names, were fluff.

Empty headed and personality free.

When he scanned a room, he couldn't tell one from another. Often, depending on the fashions of the year, he could not tell boys from girls either.

Certain names spelled death for telling kids apart. This year, in the eleven A.M. class alone, he had a Cristin, a Kierstin, and a Christine. His eight-thirty A.M. class actually included a Khrystyn. What was it with these parents who had to have designer spelling along with designer names?

Luckily, as Driver's Ed instructor, he didn't have to participate in Parents' Night. Sessions were only eight weeks and nobody—especially Mr. Fielding—felt that Driver's Ed was really a class.

Besides, what would he say to the grown-ups who had spawned these brainless little clones? "Yes, Kierstin occupies her seat well."

And most of all, what would he say to grown-ups who had actually, legally, named their daughter Rembrandt?

Rembrandt! At least the kid knew better than to use

7

the name and called herself Remy. She had a shock coming when she got her driver's license: no nicknames allowed. Her license would say Rembrandt Marland and there was no escape.

Mr. Fielding had to refer to his class record book to have the slightest idea who was sitting in the car with him. Last year he'd had each kid wear a name tag, laminated and glued to a pin. Very successful. He was doing it again this year. That way, when he turned to the blond girl in torn, faded blue jeans who looked exactly like four other blond girls in torn, faded blue jeans, he would know which was Remy and which was Kierstin. And not confuse Kierstin with Christine or Cristin.

Today he had a Post-it on his classbook, to remind himself the current driver was not part of the Cristin series. The Cristin series member was in back with a last-name-for-first-name boy and would rotate forward if and when Mr. Fielding remembered to change drivers. "Take River Road, Remy."

"River Road?" she squeaked. "It's about an inch wide!"

"It's wide enough for two cars," said Mr. Fielding. "You just have to pay attention." He did not imply that *he* had to pay attention.

He knew he was not teaching. He was merely there, and they were merely there. Time passed and then they left. Year after year he and they mindlessly drifted through an eight-week session. Then a new set of indistinguishable little clones filled the seats and wore the name tags. Sometimes he thought he should just pass out the same name tags. What would it matter if Chad wore Thad's tag? Who could tell if Darya responded to Darcy?

* * *

8

Of course, the class was way ahead of Mr. Fielding.

They had been exchanging name tags for weeks. Christine, who had not successfully merged into the eight lanes on day one, but gave up, sobbing, and tried to abandon the car at the edge of the turnpike, never took another turn. Lark usually got her name tag.

Kierstin would drive only if there were no boys along. She was palm-sweaty, migraine-headachy, and jelly-kneed behind the wheel. She was afraid of every driving decision and it showed. She didn't mind girls laughing at her, but *boys*—forget it. The class hours were required in order to register for the state driving test, but Kierstin figured practice with her mother would be enough. She usually gave her name tag to Remy.

This was one reason why Mr. Fielding could not tell his Cristin/Kierstin/Christine group apart—they were generally Remy or Lark.

Lark had unfastened her seat belt and was leaning way forward, resting her tiny chin next to Remy's shoulder. She was a committed backseat driver, monitoring RPMs, speed, following distance, and especially Mr. Fielding's instructions. "Go right," he'd say.

"No, not here," Lark would argue. "That road looks dull." Lark had high scenery standards.

"You won't even be able to enjoy the radio, Remy," said Lark relentlessly. "Your two brothers never stop yelling."

Lark was correct. Henry, who was thirteen months old, yelled without words. He offered constant shrieking opinions when he couldn't even talk yet. He had a howl that meant, "No! Never! Get a life!" and another that meant "Yes! Now! Get with the program!" Henry

9

had a full-speed personality. He'd gone straight from crawling to running, and like a new ice skater at an indoor rink, he had difficulty stopping. Taking care of Henry was like being a hockey goalie.

Mac, on the other hand, had a vocabulary, though limited. Mac's idea of a good thing to do when he grew up was sue people. It was his favorite sentence. "Let's sue 'em!" he loved to yell. Mac wanted to sue his teachers, the bus driver, the neighbors, the opposite team's coach, and everybody else on earth who ever got in his way.

The person who most got in his way was his sister, Remy.

Remy sensibly avoided the subject of her brother Mac. "Henry isn't a life sentence," she said. "He'll outgrow the car seat eventually."

"Left," said Mr. Fielding.

Remy clicked her signal and carefully studied the unfamiliar left turn. Two lanes of oncoming traffic, but there was a stoplight. She halted exactly behind the white line. The light turned green. Remy didn't give the intersection any more thought. She had the green, so what was there to think about?

Remy spun the steering wheel left and accelerated. She loved accelerating. It was so neat how you just flexed your ankle and the car sprang across the road.

"Sure, when you're in college, Henry'll be out of his car seat," said Lark. "It's Mac who won't outgrow anything." Lark turned to Morgan and added, "That subhuman stage lasts so long in boys."

Oh, to have a brother like Morgan, thought Remy. Morgan had never gone through a subhuman stage. Mr. and Mrs. Campbell were not the kind of people who would give birth to a primitive savage like Mac.

The Campbells had put in an order for blond, slim, athletic, brilliant, articulate, successful children and gotten them. Starr and Morgan Campbell were without flaw.

Remy studied Morgan in her rearview mirror. If Morgan were her brother, he would be worth keeping, which was a rarity in brothers.

And if he were her boyfriend . . .

However, boyfriends were even rarer than worthy brothers.

Regrettably, while she was observing future boyfriends, Remy did not observe the median. In spite of a gaudy yellow line painted on the curb, Remy did not notice that the road onto which she had turned was divided by a raised cement strip.

"Remy, stop!" shrieked Lark.

Remy's heart leaped. Stop for what? There were no cars aimed at her! She had the green.

"Look out!" shouted Morgan. "Turn! Pull to the right!"

Her nervous foot slammed down on the accelerator.

Mr. Fielding, of course, said nothing. Driver's Ed was largely self-taught.

Remy drove into eight vertical inches of solid cement.

She screamed. Lark screamed. Morgan groaned and slid out of sight.

The low-slung Driver's Ed vehicle was not a Bronco or Jeep designed for this. The car went up, but not across. From its underside came a horrible grinding and crashing.

Remy accelerated, because that's where her foot was —on the gas. The engine roared. *What am I doing?* she thought, doing it.

The car would be hung up on the divider. People would point and stare and laugh. They'd take videos and sell them. She'd have to pay blackmail.

In front of Morgan! Oh, please, God, where are you? Don't let me be a jerk in front of Morgan. No wonder Kierstin won't drive in front of boys. *God, get me out of this!*

The horror of being stranded in the middle of the road forced Remy's foot down even harder on the accelerator. The car lurched over the cement, scraping and tearing, leaving some of its innards behind. By now Remy was giving the car so much gas, it vaulted through the air as in a movie stunt.

She kept going. She couldn't think of anything else to do.

The engine continued to throb.

Morgan reported that it was just part of the muffler Remy had deposited on the divider. Nothing essential.

Remy's heart developed a new rhythm, like some Caribbean dance nobody had learned yet. Her fingers turned to ice and her face was a beet of shame.

"Why'd you do that?" said Mr. Fielding curiously.

"I didn't see it!" she wailed.

"What if it had been a person standing there, instead of just cement?" asked Mr. Fielding.

"I would have seen a person!"

But what if it *had* been a person? What if she'd left a *body* behind, instead of tailpipe?

She'd be a hit-and-run driver. A criminal. Leaving the scene of the accident. No excuse but a heavy foot. "Don't tell," she said urgently to Lark and Morgan.

"Of course we're telling," said Lark. "This is the best mistake yet."

* * *

Of the two types of magazines Morgan liked to look at, only car magazines were permissible in public, so he kept a *Car and Driver* with him at all times, memorizing, studying, and yearning.

He had stood on the threshold of being sixteen ever since he could remember. He ached to be the driver. He wanted long journeys. Total freedom. Complete control. He'd leave town, leave the state, drive every turnpike in the nation from start to finish.

He had no destinations. He didn't care about destinations. He just wanted to drive. Fast.

He came from a family that specialized in yearning for things.

His father yearned for power, and was going to try to move up in the world: from statehouse to governor. His mother yearned for money, and had just become full partner in her law firm. His sister, Starr, yearned for both these things, but she called it popularity.

Starr was cruel in the way of twelve-year-old girls, going up to people on purpose and telling them their teeth were crooked, their jeans were dumb, and their jokes were pathetic. Starr was the most sought-after girl in junior high, which in Morgan's opinion was due to fear. She had terrified the other girls into submission. Starr didn't have a friend in the world; she was just popular.

Experience with Starr established that girls were awful. And yet girls were the wonderful and desirable focus of the other magazines, the ones he kept in the cellar, behind his weight-lifting equipment. Sometimes he thought even more about girls than cars.

Class, food, parents, television, music, wheels— some days he could hardly even see this stuff. The world was redolent of the possibilities that were out there, that he was not getting; that he had no idea how to get; that he was sure to mess up when he did get them.

Being so close to both Lark and Remy confused him.

Lark was a bubblehead who laughed at everything from surprise quizzes to field-trip buses that broke down five miles from a bathroom. You couldn't be with Lark without having a great time.

Lark was very slight, however, and gave off an aura of being breakable that did not appeal to Morgan.

Remy, now. Her figure had matured in seventh grade and Morgan had been studying it ever since. Remy was given to wearing sweatshirts over jeans, and her figure beneath the sweatshirt was pronounced and unmistakable. When they talked, Morgan had to discipline himself to meet her eyes instead of her curves.

Now, sitting behind her, he thought about her hair. It was absolutely straight, cut one hair at a time, each golden strand fractionally shorter than the one beneath. If he touched the shorn edge he would feel the soft back of her neck at the same time as the bristles of her cut hair.

What if he went out with Remy?

First he would have to ask her. A problem as hard to get over as cement road dividers.

Whoever he went out with, he would drive. Period. There would be no discussion on that one. Morgan didn't care one bit about equality when it came to driving.

He was grateful to Remy for being a jerk back at that intersection. He could hold it over her. Probably stretch it out for years. Now if Lark would just screw up, too, he could really wallow in his masculine superiority.

Remy's eyes filmed over, blurring the road so badly it was just a matter of moments before she drove over a second, probably pedestrian-occupied, cement divider.

"Remy, pull into that parking lot," said Mr. Fielding. "The one in front of that strip mall."

There were hundreds of strip malls. The entire world was a strip mall. Remy was too rattled to study buildings by the side of the road. "Which one?"

"That one," said Mr. Fielding helpfully.

"Put on your right turn signal," said Morgan loudly.

"Put on your left turn signal," said Lark, louder.

Remy continued straight ahead, which involved fewer choices.

I can't even choose left or right! she thought. My pulse is blowing up like fireworks over left or right. How am I going to pick a college if I can't even pick left or right?

"Calm down," said Mr. Fielding. "It's no big deal. Nobody's dead."

That was the dividing line between big deal and little deal? Death?

Remy could not transfer her foot to the brake, choose a turn signal, and pick out a mall. Like Christine she just gave up, hauled the car off the road, and sat panting on the shoulder.

"Your turn to drive . . . Christine," said Mr. Fielding.

It was a good thing Lark opened both doors for Remy. Close-callness peeled off her poise like skin from a sunburn. She got into the back with Morgan and forced herself to look over, see how big of a deal he was going to make of her pathetic driving.

Morgan was smiling his distant sweet smile. He must have learned the smile from a father in politics. It made you feel loved, but just generic love, not you in particular. Remy wanted to be loved in particular. She especially wanted kisses. She kissed her baby brother continually for practice, but a one-year-old's forehead did not count.

"You okay?" said Morgan. His voice was his father's too: warm and reassuring. Don't worry about the economy or global nightmares: just elect me and all will be well.

Don't worry about Driver's Ed and popularity: just look into my eyes and I'll make everything better.

"Oh, Morgan. You just saw me. I'm okay but I'm stupid." She wanted to cry so Morgan would comfort her, but she wanted not to cry so Morgan would think she was strong.

Morgan took her hand and tightened his muscles against her cold palm. "Calm down," he said softly. "Mr. Fielding's right. No big deal, nobody's dead."

She didn't let go of Morgan's hand. It was remarkably larger than hers. His thumb was immense. Even his hand had muscles. He had more muscle in his hand than she did in her whole arm.

She drifted into dreams of Morgan. She was now acquainted with his thumb. This would be a meaningful experience for Morgan and he would ask her out. She let herself be thrown against Morgan when Lark miscalculated cornering speed.

Morgan responded by shoving her back in place and

16

finding her seat belt for her. "You want to die?" he said disapprovingly.

No, I just want to sit in your lap.

Their faces were very close. Morgan's smile turned into a wicked grin. A junior-high-boy, worthless-younger-brother-Mac, I've-got-you-now grin. "How's Jesus?" he said.

Remy laughed.

When Remy's mother had become pregnant again at forty-four, the family had been both horrified and thrilled. Thrilled won. Medical tests assured them the baby would be a girl, so they spent months deciding on a girl's name. It had to be romantic and unusual and melodious. It had to please all four of them, since they all would have to live with it and change its diapers.

They settled on Andressa, only to have a boy. They had not spent a nanosecond on boys' names. The baby went into hospital records as Baby Boy Marland. Of course, during the Name Decision Period, they still had to call the baby something.

Remy called the baby Sweet Prince, because he was so adorable.

Mac, nauseated by what a kid would go through with a name like Sweet Prince, called him Matthew, since all the Matthews Mac knew were good athletes and fit in socially.

Remy's mother called the baby Jamie, which Dad wouldn't accept because it could also be a girl's name, while Dad held out for Jason, which Mom wouldn't accept because there were too many Jasons in the world already.

So there they were, calling this eight pounds of person Matthew or Jamie or Jason or Sweet Prince, when

17

Mr. and Mrs. Marland came to a decision out of no-where and decided on Henry.

Henry? everybody complained. You call that a name? That outdated, out-of-fashion pair of syllables?

When the baby was a few months old, Christmas arrived.

Naturally a real live baby was more desirable for the Christmas pageant than somebody's old doll. Baby Boy Marland, who that week of life slept well, took the starring role and lay placidly in a manger. Remy's mother was maybe a little too proud of Baby Boy Marland's role.

The pageant came and went. The name Jesus did not. "Night-night, Jesus," Mom would croon over the crib. "Sleep tight, Jesus."

The rest of the family certainly hoped this was a habit Mom would get rid of before they had to have her committed.

Shortly after Christmas the baby stopped sleeping, as if sleep were a vice he did not intend to have. If he ever got to sleep, he certainly didn't sleep tightly; this was the loosest-sleeping baby in America.

Now he was over a year old, and nobody had surrendered on the name front.

"Henry's pretty good," she told Morgan, "but we're name-training Mom now. Jesus is out."

"That's too bad," said Morgan. "I thought it added a little to Sunday school to have Jesus attending."

Remy thought it would add even more to have Morgan attending.

Lark went through a red light.

Brakes screamed.

Horns blared.

Single middle fingers pointed upward.

Windows rolled down.

Swear words were heard.

Lark drove quickly on. For the next intersection she began stopping several hundred feet early. They didn't get rear-ended only because there was no car behind them to do it.

Mr. Fielding said to her, "I know you saw that red light back there. You stopped."

"I know, but I forgot to stay stopped."

Morgan was delirious with pleasure. What a quote. He couldn't wait to tell the other boys. *I forgot to stay stopped.*

Masculine superiority. Nothing like it.

"My turn, Lark," he said. "Get out. Switch. We're practically back at school and I haven't had my chance."

"We're in the middle of the street, Morgan. I can't get out here."

"Nobody's behind us." Morgan leaped out of the backseat, raced around the car, ripped open the driver's door, and unlatched Lark's seat belt. In case she had not realized that he was serious, he uncurled her fingers from the steering wheel and yanked her by the elbow.

"Well! Really!" said Lark. "Just because you're afraid for your life."

CHAPTER 2

"Now, this new piece," said Mr. Willit, "is a love song. And therefore, dear chorus of mine, we will perform it lovingly."

Concert Choir regarded him nervously. The music teacher had an unfortunate tendency to embarrass them in public.

"We're going to choreograph this number. Not only will we sing," said Mr. Willit, "but right here on the risers we're going to waltz the waltz, hug the hug, and kiss the kiss." He demonstrated his air hugs and air kisses in three-four time.

Sixty-eight singers made various expressions of horror and revulsion.

"Mr. Willit," said Lark, "try to be normal."

Mr. Willit jerked dramatically to a halt. "Normal?" he cried. "Excuse me, Lark. In this room, in this gathering, did you actually use the word *normal*?"

Remy loved this stuff. Mr. Willit was always a bit player in a skit he wrote on the spot. She glanced at Morgan, to see Morgan's wonderful easy grin, but Morgan was mesmerized by the music folder in his lap, which in fact held his driver's manual, so he could study rules of the road when the tenors weren't singing.

"Look around you!" cried Mr. Willit. "Do you see any normalcy lurking?"

They imitated him, scanning the room for normal people.

"In fact," said Mr. Willit, "you students here at East Line High don't need to worry if anybody gets into Harvard. You just hope two or three of you will be normal by graduation." He looked carefully through sopranos, altos, tenors, and basses. "Normalcy is so far out of reach for you people, I fear I shall have to narrow the field." He squinted and shaded his eyes. "Aha! Morgan! Come!"

Morgan Campbell. Normal.

Morgan's parents had far greater plans for their son than normalcy. They expected straight A's, brilliance in field and gym, leadership in student government, astonishing achievement in some unusual and fascinating activity, plus a clear complexion.

Remy prayed to the God Who Restrained Music Teachers not to let Mr. Willit embarrass Morgan. Remy had a large selection of gods, each with its own specific duty in life: a god to protect her from the dark, a god to endanger Mac's existence, a god to make Morgan fall in love with her.

The chorus was delighted with Mr. Willit's choice, because Morgan was perfect and needed to be the butt of a joke.

Mr. Willit took Morgan's cheeks in his hands and turned Morgan's head left and then right for the chorus to admire. Morgan was measurably taller and wider. Mr. Willit looked like a skinny shopper buying a big garden statue.

21

19684
FICTION

"Kid," proclaimed Mr. Willit in a huge, rolling voice, "this is your year. I am going to make you normal. Nobody else here is going to achieve this pinnacle of success. *Normalcy.* Think about it, Morgan. Thank your lucky stars."

The chorus went wild. Stomping, whistling, catcalling.

"Wave at the crowds," Mr. Willit instructed. "Poor twisted little beggars. At least they have you to look up to now."

Mr. Willit taught Morgan to wave like the Royal Family. Swiveling from the wrist, so as not to tire out the whole hand.

Morgan accepted the applause with dignity.

Remy quivered with wanting him. She wanted to be his girlfriend, and get applause with him, and be applauded by him.

But he didn't glance at the sopranos on his return to his seat and when chorus ended she got swept up by Lark. The two girls arrived at Driver's Ed first. Remy was forced to sit without knowing where Morgan would be.

"Did you see the mailboxes?" said Joss.

Christine nodded. "Who's doing it?"

Mailbox baseball had swept the city. Hundreds of mailboxes had been trashed during the night.

"Nobody knows," said Lark, making it sound as if she, of course, knew perfectly well.

Chase and Morgan came in together, too broad to fit through the door. Morgan dropped back, and Remy's heart skipped thinking of how much the boys had grown this year. Why couldn't Morgan participate in a bare-chested spectator sport?

"They must have been at it all night. It'd take hours

to do that much damage," said Chase. He and Morgan yanked out chairs opposite Joss and Remy and dropped boy-style onto their seats, as heavily as elephants with broken legs.

Good view. Thank you, God of True Love.

"No, it wouldn't," said Taft. "You'd have two guys in the bed of the pickup truck, swinging alternately, and you could cover the city in no time."

"Were you in on it?" asked Christine.

"Certainly not," said Taft indignantly.

"Anyway, that's not how you play," said Cristin. "It really is just like baseball. One person at a time swings. Three strikes and you're out."

Vandalism was supposedly a boys' activity. Did Cristin speak from experience? This certainly put Cristin in a new light.

Remy could not imagine herself smashing mailboxes. She would probably laugh hysterically the first time she picked up the bat, and then of course, the God of Her Mother Watching would descend and make it impossible to do anything even remotely bad. The God of Her Mother Watching was very powerful.

"Lots of idiots go out and paint rocks with their initials," Lark said. "Or paint the sides of bridges. Or in this case, smash mailboxes. The urge for immortality, of course."

Remy was surprised by this little speech. She took her eyes off Morgan long enough to check out Lark's smile. Small, stretched—a rubber band demanding to be shot. "You know what I'm thinking?" said Lark.

The class listened. Lark usually had good ideas.

"Let's all take signs. I love signs. Let's make it a class game."

"I love signs too. I've got a BIKE PATH collection," said

23

Chase. "I've got six of 'em lined up on my wall next to my trophies. I'm on the bike team, you know."

They knew. Chase could be very tiresome about his old bike team.

"I don't have any signs, but I've always wanted WEYMOUTH ROAD," said Alexandra Weymouth. She resembled her name: elegant and historic. She had golden-blond hair like Remy's, but long, swingy, and better. "Weymouth Road isn't named for my family, of course. We're not from around here." She shook her head, amused by the concept of being from around here. "Still, I'd like the sign."

Alexandra swung her golden hair in Morgan's direction. "Let's us get WEYMOUTH ROAD this weekend, Morgan."

Alexandra was gorgeous. Morgan was as crazy about her as he was about most girls. Alexandra wanted his company? He should have been thrilled. Instead he felt panicky. "I don't have a car," he pointed out.

Lark laughed at him. "Morgan's afraid of girls, Alexandra," said Lark.

This was the kind of thing Starr said, to bring people to their knees and obey her every whim.

I'm not afraid of girls, thought Morgan. I adore girls. I think of girls every waking and sleeping minute. Sometimes I even have to wake up in the night to think about them more.

Alexandra left her chair and sat right in Morgan's lap.

Morgan had no idea what to do. He couldn't flirt, or laugh, or even enjoy it.

"All boys are afraid of girls," said Lark. "Has anybody actually heard of a girl having a date?"

"This is a school for sick puppies," agreed Christine. "Nobody dates. You hear rumors, but you never actually come across it."

Alexandra wrapped herself around Morgan. If he blinked, his lashes would graze her chest. Less chest than Remy, but still, a chest he was more than willing to graze.

"In fact," put in Cristin, "the most that actually happens when two kids 'go together' is that now and then the boy 'lets' the girl go with him to a movie."

The girls all groaned and nodded. The boys all listened carefully. They knew they knew nothing.

"Last week," said Lark, "I shouted at Morgan, *Take me, Morgan! I am yours! Name your time and place!* And Morgan says, *Chemistry, fourth period, on the lab table next to the Bunsen burner.* I, of course, show up. Morgan, of course, skips class."

The class laughed.

Morgan blushed even though Lark was making this up completely. Tentatively Morgan moved his hands. Alexandra gave him a half smile that could have meant anything.

Remy was beside herself. How could Alexandra move in so fast? It wasn't fair, but then, Alexandra was too beautiful for fairness to be in the picture. Remy would never have more of Morgan than hand-holding in the back of the Driver's Ed car.

Morgan's hand crept around Alexandra, while Remy prayed to the God of True Love to make Morgan want her body more than Alexandra's.

"So! Okay!" said Lark. Tiny as she was, she had a drill sergeant's voice. "Signs! Our class activity. Our own personal Driver's Ed special. Here's the rule: Nobody gets a license without taking a sign first."

"Awww-right!" said Chase. "I'm in."

"I've been in for years," said Taft. "You know Lighthouse Lane, with the cute little wooden lighthouse sign? We've got three of them. My brother took it for his college dorm, they replaced it, my sister took that one for her college dorm, and when they replaced it again, I took it for my room."

They all laughed except Morgan, whose mind was on other things, and Christine, who said, "Cut it out. I'm dropping this class if you really start that. I'm not getting into trouble."

"You just want an excuse to quit Driver's Ed," said Alexandra.

"Don't be a flea bite, Christine," said Lark. "Nobody would get into trouble. Everybody takes signs."

Mr. Fielding wandered in and conversation stopped for once. Mr. Fielding only represented authority, and had not yet actually exerted any, but you never knew. "All right, class. Joanne, Carson, and Chrystal will drive today."

Since the class did not include anybody named Joanne, Carson, or Chrystal, there should have been a pause, but nobody missed a beat. Lark, Remy, and Morgan leaped right up.

Even though the same three had driven yesterday, nobody interfered. Instead they high-fived each other and made notations in their notebooks.

Driver's tests were already being scheduled. Mr. Fielding would actually escort to the Motor Vehicle Bureau kids who had driven only once. The class had placed serious bets on whether the single-time drivers would pass.

Mr. Fielding headed out through the library with Lark nipping at his heels like a small ill-behaved dog, claiming to be Chrystal, and begging to be first to drive.

"You be Joanne," Remy said to Morgan.

"Wave to us, Joanne," said Taft, grinning.

Morgan waved like the Royal Family, swiveling the wrist, so as not to tire the whole hand.

"Queen Joanne the Normal," said Taft.

Lark drove.

"River Road," said Mr. Fielding.

Morgan sat in back with Remy, staring out the window because looking at Remy made him nervous.

It was surprising how much country there was left, and how close to the city it lay. Their city had become a cement amoeba, splitting endlessly into more cities. Enormous office complexes, huge tracts of housing developments, miles of strip malls. Nevertheless, the buildings and developments ended more quickly than he would have thought.

River Road grew narrower and the woods closed in. They'd had a dull and speedy autumn. Leaves hardly even turned colors, just made a brown exit from life. Morgan did not find the scrawny woods attractive.

A square yellow sign was set diagonally on its tall metal staff. THICKLY SETTLED, said fat black print.

"Don't you love that?" said Lark. "You never see a THICKLY SETTLED sign in town, where it really is thickly settled. You see THICKLY SETTLED out in the woods, where it isn't settled at all, never mind thickly." Lark counted driveways as she hurtled by. "There are exactly four houses here, so naturally the highway department throws up that desperately needed sign. THICKLY SETTLED."

Morgan had certainly never given any thought to sign placement. He didn't now either. Queen Joanne the Normal. It made him laugh, and want to wave at the crowds again.

THICKLY SETTLED vanished as Lark whipped by, much too fast. She lucked out. There was no oncoming traffic and she didn't career off the road. "THICKLY SETTLED," Lark announced, "would be perfect in my bedroom."

Morgan tried to picture a girl's bedroom in which a large yellow THICKLY SETTLED sign would be perfect. His sister's bedroom was the only girl's room he knew, and he didn't know it well. Starr killed people who went unasked into her bedroom, and she certainly never asked her brother there. Starr had not quite left her Barbie and Ken stage, and the room was full of dolls and dollhouses and doll accessories, with Barbie outfits hanging from tiny closet rods mounted in a pink-painted jog in the wall.

"How will you get THICKLY SETTLED?" Morgan asked. They had to be five miles beyond city limits. Obviously nobody had a license, although Remy had a car.

Four months ago, when his sixteenth birthday arrived, Morgan had been absolutely completely positive he would get a car. His parents were rich; they had a BMW and a Range Rover; he had dropped many hints of Miata convertibles. He wasn't sure he'd get the Miata, but he certainly knew he'd get a car.

He was wrong.

A VCR for his bedroom was their idea of a decent present. As if he ever wanted to stay in his room again! "Sixteen equals cars!" he wanted to yell at his parents. "Give me a car!"

But he didn't.

He rarely spoke to his parents at all.

The years he was thirteen, fourteen, and fifteen, he could love them only when they were out of sight. Especially his mother. Just being in the room with her made him crazy. He wanted to scream and swear and disobey, but rarely did. He stayed silent and waited until she left, or he could.

Finally, this year, he could be in the room with them. He wasn't talking yet, but he was close. He was now at the stage of thinking of things he would say to his father if he were talking to his father. Receiving a car would have been a good conversation starter.

Now his hopes rested on the morning he got his driver's license. They hadn't wanted to start carrying expensive car insurance before he was actually driving, that was all. Or have in the garage the temptation of a car he couldn't yet touch.

That's the plan, he told himself. Day of my test, I'll come home and find my own car waiting in the driveway. That new metallic red I like. Actually, it doesn't have to be red. Or a Miata. It just has to have Wow-factor. No clunkers. No wide-bodies.

Remy recrossed her legs the opposite way. Her jeans made an audible friction rub. Morgan stared at the jeans-crossing. Talk about Wow-factor.

"The bolts are probably rusted together," said Lark.

Morgan struggled back to the subject of signs.

"And I'd need help taking the sign off the post."

Is she serious? thought Morgan. She really wants a dumb sign? He could never tell when girls were serious.

"It probably really is thickly settled, Lark," Remy pointed out. "The thick part is just hidden by trees. Probably the neighbors participate in Neighborhood Watch, and they'll be watching. They'll see you take it and they'll write down your plate number."

"And then it's prison for Lark," said Morgan. "But prisons are THICKLY SETTLED. The sign could still be useful."

Lark had a very small mouth, as if her lips had been designed for some other face entirely. She tightened her tiny lips into a pout. "You don't go to prison for stealing signs, Queen Joanne," said Lark. "It's a little itty bit of wood and paint. All you do is pay a fine."

"How do you know?" said Morgan, genuinely interested. Did Lark have experience at this? She had experience, according to high school rumor, at everything else.

"Joel and I used to take them all the time," said Lark. "It's so fun. I've got YIELD and DANGEROUS CURVE and NO RIGHT ON RED and three sizes of arrows. And then Joel moved away and my parents wouldn't let me go to Atlanta with him."

They had reached the end of River Road and were at the north entrance of the bypass. Lark merged perfectly into the southbound traffic, because there wasn't any, and headed back to the city.

"You were fourteen when you went out with Joel," said Remy. "How could you possibly have thought your parents would let you go to Atlanta with him?"

"Because I was fourteen," said Lark. "Fourteen is dumb and ignorant. Now, Morgan, I want that sign. I need THICKLY SETTLED to round out my collection."

Morgan did not know why girls had to chatter all the time. How were you supposed to have a decent daydream about the various Wow-factors of life when they babbled about their personal history?

"Morgan," said Lark, "you're a good friend of Nicholas Budie, aren't you?"

* * *

They were nearly at the exit for the school.

Mr. Fielding gazed at the high enticing sign of a Dunkin' Donuts. He was as separated from his students as if he had gotten out of the car and gone for coffee.

Morgan felt invaded. He had not been friends with Nickie for years and yet Lark immediately identified his past.

Fifth and sixth grade had been spent playing with Nickie. Nickie was a year older, which meant nothing until Nickie entered junior high, acquiring friends from other parts of town and demanding to be called Nicholas. Nickie didn't "play" anymore. Morgan just annoyed him; Morgan was a baby.

What a shock to find his friend wanted him to dry up and blow away. Morgan came back again and again for punishment, somehow believing that this time, Nickie would want his company. Nickie did not.

Nickie, now a high school senior, had a car. It was a heavy, featureless old Buick, the kind women who play bridge and men who sell office supplies might drive. But did it ever have an engine! That car could go.

You could fit three in front because it didn't have a divided seat, and in back you could cram four if you wanted. Nickie usually wanted. The ultimate popularity test was to have a full car at all times to all destinations, so Nickie gave everybody rides.

Even Morgan.

Morgan was ashamed to see how willingly he rushed back into friendship. He must have been hoping all this time that Nickie would let him back, as if Nickie were a secret clubhouse and now at last Morgan could join.

Nickie loved being the one with the license and the car. He might have been Captain in the army, with the brightest uniform and the shiniest medals. And his passengers might have been slaves taken in battle, eager to line up and please the master.

All these thoughts made Morgan slightly sick.

He said to Lark, "Yeah, I know Nicholas Budie."

Lark's eyes were shining, and she tucked her lips in like sheets, as if keeping plans inside. "Do you think Nicholas would drive?"

Remy knew what sign she'd take.

MORGAN ROAD.

Wouldn't it be neat to have the street sign with the name of the boy on whom she had a crush?

Of course, if Nickie Budie drove, Remy wouldn't be allowed to go. Nobody's parents approved of Nickie Budie, even though now he was called Nicholas, which sounded more reliable.

But she couldn't take MORGAN ROAD when Morgan was around anyway. Any boy, at such visible evidence of serious crush, would flee the country.

Would Nicholas drive . . . ?

When they were ten and eleven, Morgan Campbell and Nickie Budie were in love with roads.

They'd sneak out after dark, follow the road out of sight of their houses, and wrestle on the white line in the middle of the street. When headlights appeared, they had to dive for cover, as if oncoming cars were bombers in war.

They could not hide like girls, protecting themselves, worrying about clothes, scratches, brambles, or broken glass. It was imperative to dive into the ditch without checking out the bottom.

Extra points if you actually dove onto rusty cans or

an old hubcap or a pile of sharp rocks and hurt yourself. Blood was good.

He remembered his mother's exasperation at the torn clothes and the wonderful lies he told because you could hardly explain to your mother that your hobby was playing in the traffic after dark.

Morgan and Nickie played chase too. The point was that neither boy could slow down once the chase began. Not for anything. Not for fences or dogs. Not for backyards or traffic, brooks or swamps.

Morgan loved being the one who fled. He felt criminal, sick with the sense that if caught, he would be jailed or thrashed. It had a curious appeal. But he also loved being the one who chased. Closing in on Nickie —knowing that in a moment he'd throw the other boy to the ground—that he'd be the winner and the power.

Chicken and chase had faded away, their place taken by socially approved games like baseball and football. The swamps and the woods had vanished in the last few years anyway, infilled and built upon, seamlessly part of the vast new city.

Memory came back, sweaty and enclosing, as if Lark had tossed Morgan back into a soup of running and chasing, screaming and catching.

"Yeah," he said, "Nicholas would drive."

CHAPTER 3

Current Events was last period.

Morgan hoped there would be a film. He wanted to sit in the dark and think about girls and cars, not the world. Unless the topic was war. Morgan loved war. He wished he could be in the army.

In September they had drawn names of nations at war so each student would have his own personal conflict to report on. Morgan got Guatemala and was bored and annoyed. Guatemala's civil war was just lying there, as inactive as last century's volcano.

Morgan wanted danger: Beirut danger, Azerbaijan danger, Israeli danger. He was also attracted to mountain danger: Yugoslavian and Afghanistan danger. But nobody would trade. They said he'd gotten enough trades in Driver's Ed. How were you supposed to find danger in the world Morgan had been born occupying? Bosnian sixteen-year-olds got to use machine guns and divert snipers and rescue their families.

It was a sad situation when the most dangerous thing in a boy's world was Lark going through a red light.

"Hey, Rembrandt?" said Joss. "You do your homework? Can I copy it?"

"Call me Rembrandt and die," snapped Remy. "No, you can't copy my homework. I'm not giving it away; I worked on it all night long." This was a blatant lie. She had worked fifteen minutes, and been on the phone with Lark at the time.

"All right, already," said Joss, pouting.

"You aren't supposed to talk so loud when somebody asks you about copying," said Morgan, grinning at Remy.

Remy dissolved under his grin. Where had Alexandra found the courage to jump into his lap, and how could Remy find it too?

"So," said Lark, after class and before the run to the bus. This left them perhaps ninety seconds for a conversation. "Is it a date?"

Remy, as so often happened around Lark, felt dense. Lark always seemed to be ahead of the subject or else felt the subject did not need to be named. "Is what?" said Remy.

"The four of us," said Lark irritably. "You, me, Morgan, and Nicholas. The first sign expedition."

Sign. The word sounded familiar. Vestiges of sign conversation came back to Remy.

Remy's memory kept completely different conversations than her best friend's. Lark invariably remembered more, and in greater detail, as if she were preparing evidence for trials. When Remy thought back on conversations, they had a dreamy quality, as if she hadn't been there, but had gotten it thirdhand.

Lark moved on. "What do you say, Morgan?"

Say yes, Morgan, Remy prayed. She didn't want to say it first. It sounded greedy, or too sure of herself.

Morgan paused so long that she had time to pray to the God of True Love, and also time to know that the God of True Love was elsewhere today.

"Date," said Morgan finally.

Blackness and stars filled her mind like fainting. "Date," she seconded, monitoring her voice to keep out greed and sureness. Casual. That was the thing. Boys didn't like you unless you were relaxed about them.

Lark immediately gave orders, with twice the sureness Remy had omitted. "Tell your parents you're going to watch movies at my place," she instructed. "Parents don't mind seeing the sign in your room, but they don't like knowing ahead of time that you're going to take it."

Mr. Willit had school-bus supervision, which meant standing on the sidewalk trying not to get bruised or otherwise damaged as the high school emptied its eight hundred teenagers. "Yeah, Chase!" he bellowed. "Awright, Joss! Go, Remy!"

He loved his kids. He loved their names. Rembrandt Marland. It killed him. Who would name a daughter Rembrandt? Only a woman named Imogene. Rembrandt and Jesus in the same family. Perhaps Mac was secretly named Napoleon.

Making Morgan normal had been great fun. Next week Mr. Willit would make Remy normal. Then he'd mix voice parts and subtly arrange Remy and Morgan next to each other. He loved matchmaking.

Nicholas Budie slouched by. Mr. Willit averted his

eyes. He was committed to the belief that all kids were great, and even if they weren't, every rotten kid had potential.

Nickie got in the way of this equation.

Once Nickie'd gotten that Buick, he began running over animals. He had a personal roadkill count. He liked wandering pets best. If they wore a collar, Nickie drove out of his way to get them. In school he liked to torment wheelchair students. Even terrific kids like Morgan Campbell just barely balanced the existence of dirtbags like Nickie Budie.

The buses were beginning to pull out, long yellow beads on a strung-too-close chain. Morgan Campbell charged out of school with seconds to go before his bus departed.

"Want a ride, Morgan?" yelled Nickie Budie.

Morgan got in Nickie's car.

Something in Mr. Willit faded.

Morgan ran in the door just before dinner, which in a household as busy as the Campbells' was timed to the minute.

The Campbells' kitchen was immense. Burnished steel and polished granite, it was state-of-the-art, for gourmet cooks and brilliant dinner parties. Mostly it oversaw the pouring of Cheerios into bowls. It opened into a blaze of glass walls and skylights, a towering fireplace and several comfy couches. The huge TV could be hidden by remote-controlled wooden panels but if any Campbells were home, the TV was on, and the panels rarely closed.

He knew his father had definitely decided to run for governor when he saw two more televisions and a second VCR lined up on the room-long hearth. This way his father could see how the media covered every event, especially his. Rafe Campbell, Governor. Morgan approved of his father's name. Rafe. Stronger and more interesting than his own. He visualized the TV ads and the store posters.

"Hello, son," said his father cheerfully. "How was your day?"

Morgan looked at the father he was so proud of and had nothing to say to him. The minute he faced Dad, his thoughts evaporated, leaving no trace, as if he had never had a thought, and perhaps never would. "Okay." He shrugged.

His father was instant tired. Like instant coffee. He turned from his son to the televisions. On TV they always looked into your eyes.

Starr made up for her brother's silence, spewing junior high gossip throughout dinner. The family sat silently under the submachine-gun fire of Starr's chatter.

He thought of Remy. Who cared about that silly sign Lark wanted? It was an easy first date. He hadn't even had to ask.

Was he ready for this?

He had to be ready. He'd been thinking about it for millions of hours.

His parents had a meeting tonight; they always had a meeting tonight. In another hour he'd be in the backseat of a big, comfortable car with Remy Marland. Holding more than her hand. Touching the golden hair and exploring the fabulous figure.

"So, son," said his father, mouth happy around the edges, "what's making you smile?"

"Nothing," said Morgan.

His father's pleasure disappeared.

"You realize," said Starr, flipping two TVs off and turning the third to *Wheel of Fortune*, "this means we'll take up church again."

"Huh?"

"People running for office always go to church, dummy," said Starr.

Church. He had almost forgotten church. Now that he was sixteen, Morgan could not ditch out after the first hymn and go to Sunday school. He'd have to hear sermons and everything. Mrs. Willit was such a goody-goody. Her sermons put Morgan in a coma. Every time Morgan saw terrific, funny Mr. Willit next to that overly excited wife of his, he could not imagine what had brought those two together.

Remy always went to church.

Maybe he would sit with her.

No, in the incomprehensible world of women, that probably meant he'd have to marry her.

Mom and Dad popped back in momentarily, resplendent in their Important Meeting Clothes. Morgan felt the familiar surge of pride in them, the intense love for them, and then the need to turn away and show nothing.

His parents tried to kiss him good-night. He presented his face but did not kiss back.

"Good night, now," said his father, and the rules poured out: rules about snacks and bedtime and homework. Morgan and Starr nodded and waved, and Mom and Dad were gone.

"I won't mind church if I get lots of new clothes," said Starr.

Morgan would mind church no matter what he wore. How about if he took up a committee? Dad could get out of anything by claiming a committee meeting. If actually forced to attend, he'd just delegate the work to somebody else.

Committees, however, were for grown-ups.

How could Morgan occupy himself during a year of church while his father ran for office? "I'll probably be running the Christmas pageant," said Morgan. That'd keep him busy for the next six weeks, anyway, and possibly he'd be allowed to claim exhaustion throughout January.

Starr moved right in. "I'm your sister," she said, "and that means I get to be a king."

Morgan said nothing, but casually picked up his jacket and wandered toward the front of the house to watch for Nicholas.

"You're supposed to stay home and do homework!" yelled Starr.

Morgan said nothing.

"I'm telling!" yelled Starr.

"Fine," said Morgan. "You can be a king." Typical Starr. Get to Bethlehem using blackmail.

Nickie had grown much taller, but no wider. Toothpick thin, he was in need of a major shopping trip. His pant legs were too short and hairy wrists stuck out of his sleeves like mistakes. His torso seemed left over from junior high, while his legs had become pro-basketball length. Facial features that had been cute in elementary school were now ratlike.

Morgan got in front with Nickie. He felt uncomfortable with Nickie; sort of nervous. I'm twice his strength, thought Morgan. I could hold both his skinny wrists in one hand. Nickie is nothing.

His edginess lay light as mist, fogging his comprehension of the night.

They took a main drag, Warren Street, lined with corporate headquarters, major banks, and office buildings. Each had its own campus, neat clumps of white birch and reflecting pools with fountains. Vast parking lots were disguised by slender strips of woods.

They passed the high school, which was indistinguishable from the offices except for a huge signboard in front.

!PZZA DAY TUES!
!BRNG CLB MONEY!
!RED/WH SWTSHRTS 4 SALE!
!PSATS NEXT WKND!

There weren't enough vowels to go around, but apparently an excess of exclamation points.

"You going to ask her out?" said Nicholas.

Morgan did not know whether Nicholas meant Lark or Remy, so he shrugged rather than commit himself.

"You could do better," warned Nicholas.

Morgan shrugged his eyebrows, to say they were only girls, after all, no big deal.

But it was a big deal, and Nickie's opinion mattered. Dating was not just asking a girl out. It was asking out a girl who met other people's standards.

They stopped at the Marland house and Remy, who must have been watching for them, ran lightly and surefootedly across the yard. She was an athlete who consistently played the wrong sports for her skills, so she always came off substandard. She sure met Morgan's standards, though.

But Morgan and Nickie were in front, and Remy, seeing the pair of them, opened the back door. So he was not squashed up hot and wonderful next to Remy. Could not even see her unless he rotated uncomfortably, which was more effort than he wanted Nickie to see.

Remy had gone on a shopping binge—a tray of sparkling eye shadows, a new tube of ultrathick mascara, more lip gloss colors.

Of course it was a lie that makeup could change your life, and even when she paid for the makeup, she knew it was a lie, but she didn't care; she would try this new stuff and see if it was still a lie.

Mac had watched her getting ready, keeping up a running commentary on how useless the effort was.

Her brother Mac had all the signs of growing up to be pond scum like Nickie Budie. The kind who would steal signs in a heartbeat. Nickie, in fact, had probably outgrown the stealing of signs and was even now busily concealing stolen car phones.

Remy was the kind of little kid that when she was bad and her mother glared at her and began to count, "One! Two!" Remy was so terrified of what would happen if Mom got to "Three!" she raced to do whatever she had been told.

Mac was the kind of little kid that when Mom counted, "One! Two!" Mac got into the spirit of the thing and yelled along with her, "Three! Four!" and never once considered what kind of punishment he would get.

It wasn't as if Mom and Dad gave in. Once Mac was so rotten and worthless, Mom and Dad took away his television privileges. He went on being rotten and worthless.

Mom and Dad took away his radio. He went on being rotten and worthless. They took away telephone privileges, and then he was confined to his room, and no matter what Mom and Dad did to him, Mac went right on being rotten and worthless.

"What do we do now?" Dad said to Mom one night. "Take away his furniture? Leave him with nothing but a mattress?"

Then it dawned on them it was the mattress Mac loved. Lying awake on the bed doing nothing was Mac's favorite pastime. So they took away the mattress and after two nights sleeping on the floor Mac began to shape up.

Why can't I have a brother like Morgan Campbell? thought Remy. And then, more sensibly, thought, Since when do I want Morgan to be my brother?

When the car pulled up Remy felt like cookie dough. She was soft and sugary with nerves and delight. "Bye, Mom." Remy rushed out before her mother saw who was driving. "We'll be at Lark's watching movies. Don't worry. My homework's all done."

Her pleasure vanished when she reached the car. Nickie's ratlike eyes stared straight through the windshield instead of turning toward the person getting in his car. His arms were as thin as crossed broomsticks. Whitish hair oozed out of his head. Nickie Budie was truly a scarecrow.

Morgan was facing her, but motionless. Eyes wide and somehow calculating.

There was something awful and wrong about how the boys sat. Her heart suddenly leapt in panic, her mouth went dry, and she climbed in back, grateful that Lark would be picked up next.

Unlike everybody else Lark lived in a high-rise apartment complex. Residents' cars were parked underground. No earth had been left unpaved. Not a tree and not a bush interrupted the flow of stone and pavement. Every one of the hundreds of windows was covered by shades. The immense buildings gave no sense of being occupied.

No tiny gauzy Lark flew toward them.

Nickie leaned on the horn long and hard, which hadn't seemed so bad in front of a single house but was stupid in front of all these apartments.

"Go get her," Nickie said, neither to Morgan nor Remy, just being obnoxiously clear that the driver did not run errands. Remy opened her door without speaking and crossed the pavement to Lark's building.

Mixed in with Remy's crush on Morgan was a queer nausea. A kind of knowledge that she was in trouble. She was going as fast as a car, and would crash like metal.

Good, thought Morgan. When the girls come back, I'll get the seating right.

He watched Remy enter the outer lobby and try the interior door. Of course it didn't open. She rang the apartment from the bell board and talked into a house phone. After a few minutes Remy came back alone.

Morgan flung open the front door and edged over against Nickie to make space for Remy right next to him. He felt feverish.

"Isn't Lark dressed yet?" demanded Nicholas.

"She can't come. Her mother's getting the flu and she has to stay home and help."

Morgan found it difficult to imagine Lark heating chicken soup or soothing a headachy brow. But he forgot Lark instantly. Remy was extremely nervous. She sat gingerly next to Morgan, trying to thin herself and not touch him. Morgan reached over her lap and hung on to the handle of her door, slamming it satisfyingly and letting his arm brush over Remy on the way back. The control panel buzzed like hornets, demanding that the seat belt be closed.

"She says bring her the sign anyway," said Remy.

Nicholas drove off too fast, making the tires whine, while Morgan and Remy fussed with the single seat belt.

It was long enough to go around them both.

THICKLY SETTLED was on the curve of a sharp downward slope, deep in the woods. A few hundred yards into the curve the road would pass a couple of houses crowded by the edge of a brook. But here, although a new road had been cut into the woods for a future subdivision, no house had ever been built. No streetlights, no house lights, and only occasional headlights penetrated the dark.

Authority existed as it never had when Morgan and Nickie leapt into ditches at the sight of distant headlights. This time Authority was Police, and Authority could arrest them, in possession of stolen public property.

Morgan was amazed to find how much this appealed to him. Not *getting* caught, of course. But taking the *risk* of getting caught.

Morgan battled nausea and excitement.

If his parents knew . . . Well, he wouldn't tell. And there'd be no evidence. Lark was getting the sign, after all.

Remy was crowded next him. She wasn't shrinking anymore. He could feel her muscles relaxing, one by one, as she let herself lean on him.

The whole length of his thigh was tight against the whole length of hers. He couldn't feel much. Denim jeans were like armor.

Morgan slipped his hand across her lap until he found her hand. Curling his fingers around, he stroked the soft inner cup of her palm with his thumb. Right away he wanted more, and put his hand on the back of her neck, touching the bristly back of her hair. It did not feel the way he had expected: it was silk.

Remy Marland was deep in a heady, vibrating excitement. The utter and complete joy of being sandwiched so tightly up against Morgan made all else irrelevant.

"We'll park here," said Nicholas. He backed into the unpaved opening that would have been the exit from the housing development, if it had ever been built.

How silent the night was.

No underlying noise: no refrigerators humming, no radio, car, or plane. No coffee perking, computer printing, or baby brother crying.

And so dark.

No moon and few stars.

Nickie got out first. Morgan, who was in the middle, had to wait till Remy got out. Remy hated being outside the car. The night seemed to have a personality of its own. Soft and suffocating.

Lark had simply decided not to come. Why? Was

this part of Lark's master plan for Remy's romance? Or did Lark know something Remy didn't? Lark always knew something Remy didn't.

I want to go home, thought Remy, and immediately forgot the thought, because Morgan touched her again, his hot hand at the nape of her neck, having her silent permission to touch her there.

"Come on," said Nickie irritably.

The boys were armed.

Signs were fastened down to make taking them difficult. On most road signs, after the town crew tightened the bolt, they hammered the extending tip upward to prevent unscrewing. A simple crescent wrench probably would not do.

They had a ratchet, therefore, a hacksaw, and a bolt cutter.

All three walked softly, as if creeping through an occupied house.

Nickie's child-thin shoulders and straw hair were outlined like a cartoon by the flashlight Remy held. Morgan was much wider than Nickie—football-tackle wide. Fantasy and hope for every girl in school.

We're stealing, thought Remy.

The word landed on her like a mosquito. She actually physically brushed it away. It's just a sign, she reminded herself. A silly old sign warning drivers who don't use this road about a population that doesn't live here.

The boys got to work. Remy hung in the shadows.

Anyway, I'm not really doing this. They're really doing this. I'm just here. It isn't as if we're taking money. Or hurting anybody.

A car was coming. Its engine splattered the silent night.

47

Fear filled her mouth like a spoonful of peanut butter, sealing her shut, preventing speech and breathing.

"Don't worry about the car," said Nicholas. "You can do anything you want. Nobody ever stops."

"What if it's cops?" whispered Morgan.

Nicholas mocked him. "It won't be cops, little boy. Who would patrol here? Just keep on working."

Headlights exposed them against the black pavement. Remy felt as if she were on an operating table, naked, her heart lying open.

It's just a road sign, she said to herself. It's hardly even wrong.

The car did not slow down, but shot past as if it had no driver, was a robotized vehicle on its way to another world.

The sign came down easily. The bolt had not been hammered up after all, and the wrench did the job. Remy was amazed at how large the sign was. It didn't look like much when you drove by. Nickie carried the tools while Morgan took the sign. Nickie popped the Buick's trunk. When Morgan dropped THICKLY SETTLED down, Christmas-tree needles from last year jumped up off the carpet pile.

Nickie got back in the driver's seat. Morgan opened the door for Remy and she almost got in, but sitting in the middle meant touching Nickie. She nodded for Morgan to go in first.

Nickie saw. He drove off with a screaming spurt, undoubtedly leaving tire marks.

Remy told herself that nobody was going to photograph the tread stains. Nobody would investigate who had taken THICKLY SETTLED. They would just put up a new THICKLY SETTLED.

She tried not to think about what could have gone wrong, reminding herself that nothing had.

The Buick surged onto the highway, seventy miles an hour by the time it got to the top of the entrance ramp. Morgan sucked in his breath. Nickie was a very aggressive driver. He expected the world to move over for him, and so far it had. It did again. Morgan let the air back out of his lungs.

"So, Miss Marland," said Nickie tauntingly. The edge of his voice was like a paper cut. "What's your pleasure?"

A sentence Morgan's father used at political gatherings when he wanted action. Morgan had a brief picture of Dad's reaction if he could see his son now.

Remy's grip on Morgan tightened. Morgan felt the fine, thin bones of her fingers. She was afraid of Nickie. *Don't worry, Remy, I'm between you and Nickie. I'll take care of you. I know what a gutter rat he is. We'll never waste our time with him again.*

He could never say these things to Remy anymore than he could ever talk to his father. But he could act on them.

"Actually," Remy said, "there is a Morgan Road." He knew her eyes were blue, but in the dark there was no color. Just intensity. "We could get the street sign of Morgan Road," she whispered.

Morgan's heart left earth so fast, he jet-lagged. She wanted a Morgan Road sign? How much could he read into that? His lips and cheek did brush her hair. Soft as a down quilt, as if he could bury himself there. Morgan's fantasies smothered him.

"Where's Morgan Road?" said Nickie. "We can

49

probably just unscrew it. That's the way street-name signs are. It'll be up high to stop us, but we can stand on the roof of this baby. This is a strong car. Use it like truck."

Neither passenger heard a word.

Remy loved taking MORGAN ROAD.

Fearful as she was of cop cars, neighbors, or wandering German shepherds, she wanted the expression in Morgan's eyes to continue.

All her reading and all her observations had convinced Remy that you could never tell. You could not look at a boy and see if he cared about you.

Wrong.

One look at Morgan Campbell and you could see that he was gone. *Gone.* What a lovely expression. Morgan Campbell was gone . . . on Remy Marland.

Laughter erupted in Remy's chest, as if she had been carbonated. Bottled with love.

She stood on the roof of the Buick, Morgan holding her ankles and Nickie telling her which way to turn the sign—"Don't be such a girl," he accused her, "unscrew counterclockwise"—but in the end she couldn't turn it and had to change places with Morgan. Morgan finally wrenched it free and they leapt, laughing joyfully, into the car.

And kissed.

The kiss was easy and unplanned. Sweet and perfect.

Instead of kissing again, Remy turned away from Morgan, and got silly and flirty.

He loved it.

They had a second kiss eventually, and then Morgan kissed her throat and cheeks. They tried to keep their eyes open to admire each other, but couldn't. It was too much. You could feel or you could see, but not both.

Like driving, thought Remy. I just need practice.

The vision of Remy in the car with him changed the map of Morgan's driving daydream as if he had changed countries or languages.

Distance didn't matter. Going toward the horizon didn't matter.

Holding her hand while he drove, and stopping somewhere they could be alone, was what mattered.

Nickie stopped a mile from the high school at the corner of Cherry and Warren.

Cherry Road was a surprise in the dark, as if it sometimes went elsewhere and just for tonight had been rolled out here. It was narrow and almost invisible.

It was nine forty-five. They had been out two hours. Warren Street's six lanes usually swarmed with traffic, but by now it had just the occasional car, as if Warren were just an occasional road.

"Cops just went by on Warren," said Nickie. "We got time, they won't double back for a while."

They parked up close. People had tried to take this sign before. Not bolted with two bolts to a single pole, it was fastened by four bolts on two double channel poles. One bolt had been cut through, its flat edge now rusty. Somebody else had used a hacksaw and gotten halfway through one post. It was obviously a desirable sign.

The boys studied the problem.

The bolts had rusted into the sign. Not good. The cut into the pole, though, was a start.

Nickie handed Morgan the hacksaw. It made a lot of noise. Distinctive, demanding noise. But a city was noisy. Traffic, televisions, tires, sirens, and airplanes drowned it out.

The tendons of Morgan's neck stood out as he worked. Remy had stared at boys all her life, but never with this sense of possession. This knowledge that she could touch that muscle, stroke that tendon.

Nobody pulled up behind them on Cherry. Traffic on Warren flashed by so fast that each car was just a spear of light and then gone.

Morgan was dripping with sweat by the time he finally tore through both metal channels. Remy popped the trunk and Nickie dropped STOP on top of THICKLY SETTLED. The big red octagon gleamed momentarily and then Remy closed the lid hard. She and Morgan got back in front. Nickie turned on the engine, flicked the headlights up, and took off.

Remy tried to decide what to do with her sign. If MORGAN ROAD just materialized in her room, would her mother ignore this evidence? Pretend she never saw? Tell a story about how when she was a girl, she, too, took signs? It wasn't a very Marland family picture. She would have to cherish MORGAN ROAD in some hidden spot.

"Where will you put your stop sign?" Remy asked Nickie. "Won't your parents ask you about it?"

Nickie laughed. In the dark of the car Remy could not see his face. The laugh was alone, without a mouth to come out of. "My parents know nothing," said Nickie. "Never have, never will."

My parents know everything, thought Remy. Always have, always will.

52

Once home, she would have to be an actress, fend off questions and affection. Remy was not good at this, but with any luck Sweet Prince would be awake and crying at full volume, which would take the pressure off. Especially if she volunteered to lie down with the baby until he slept.

I will call him Henry from now on, she thought. Now I have a real Sweet Prince.

Morgan worried about school tomorrow. He must not stumble or flush when he saw Remy. People would read his face. Know that he had fallen in love. He had to hide these emotions. It was unthinkable that anybody should realize how he was feeling.

Or was it?

Chase's adoration for Suzi was room filling. Adam no longer talked of sports or cars, but only of Wendy. How did they do that without looking like jerks?

I didn't get a sign, he thought. Next time I'll get one. No Nickie along next time. Just Remy and me.

Logistical problems like no license and no vehicle briefly interrupted his daydream, but he threw them out.

There wasn't going to be a Remy Road anywhere. He'd have to come up with something meaningful and romantic. Whatever constituted romantic. Where could he find that out? He couldn't ask Starr, who was a predator and would probably initiate her romances by bludgeoning her victims.

"I can't leave the signs in my car," said Nickie. "My dad's going to use the Buick in the morning for errands, because it has the biggest trunk."

Nickie had just said his parents knew and noticed nothing. But Morgan didn't call him on it. Nickie was no longer on his list of interests. He shrugged. "We can put them in our garage." An assortment of ladders had been left by the builders and not once had any Campbell touched them. He'd drop the signs face backward behind the maze of stacked steps for Lark and Nickie to get later.

"I'm keeping MORGAN ROAD with me," said Remy.

Under a streetlamp, the gleam of her laugh and the sparkle of her eyes were illuminated.

He stopped worrying about school.

He stopped worrying about Nickie.

He had the girl.

All he needed now was the license and the car.

CHAPTER 4

"So," said Mac, "was it Nicholas or Morgan we were trying to impress?"

Why couldn't Mac move away or join the army? Remy needed the house to herself, so she could sing love songs at the top of her lungs and laugh wildly and dance on the ceiling.

"What were you guys doing tonight?" said Mac suspiciously.

She missed a beat. But her brother couldn't have seen her tuck MORGAN ROAD behind the bushes by the front door, or he'd have collected the sign already. He'd be waving it in the air and yelling for Mom and Dad to come see what their darling daughter had done.

She could not keep the wildly happy smile off her face and had to pirouette away from her brother, hiding the joy behind cupped hands.

Mac circled her as she danced, squinting into her eyes to gather more facts. "Since when have you gone to Lark's on a school night to see movies? You lied. Where'd you really go, Remy?"

"Out." She hung on to the voice that wanted to sing.

Sing. Chorus. Mr. Willit. Love songs. Air kisses and air hugs.

Yes! It was all true. Love wasn't just for other people or the final chapters of paperbacks. It was there, and it happened, and it was happening to Remy Marland.

She and Morgan wouldn't have to settle for air kisses now.

Mac made a big deal of studying his watch. "Ten twenty-five P.M. on a school night. And you were just . . . out? I'm usually the one who lies, Remy."

She wanted to open all the kitchen cabinets and slam the doors in rhythm. Dance on the countertop. Whack a few pots with wooden spoons, like her baby brother. *Morgan likes me.* "Go lick the parakeet-cage liner," she said to Mac.

"Aha!" said Mac. "I'm onto something here."

Before Mac could continue his interrogation, Mom and Dad joined them in the kitchen. The Marland family was snack happy. They had more junk food in their cupboards than anybody else in town. Remy had no idea why she was still thin, but certainly her mother was no longer thin.

"Hello, darling," said her mother, hugging and then standing back to admire her daughter. "Did you have fun?" She nodded approval over the earrings Remy had chosen. Remy's mother approved of everything about her. She told Remy constantly that she was the most beautiful, brilliant, talented, wonderful, interesting girl in America.

Remy had actually believed this until junior high, when the important girls made it clear that she was not.

Now I'm important! Morgan's gone on me!

"You are so beautiful tonight," said her mother.

56

I must be. Morgan would never be interested in a girl who isn't.

"She's also in love," said Mac. "Morgan or Nicholas, one."

"Morgan Campbell?" repeated Dad, grinning. "Remy, you told me you would never fall for anybody from Sunday school."

"Then it must be Nickie Budie," said Mac.

"Nicholas," corrected Remy, her cheeks flaming. "I don't even *like* Nicholas. He's a scummy dreck."

"It's Morgan, then," said Mac. "I knew that anyway. I was just testing you. I saw how you've written Remy Marland Campbell on your notepaper, pretending you're a bride and that's your new name."

Mom clapped her hands. "Oooooh, I adore Morgan. He's been a hunk since first grade. And I'm very fond of his parents. I wouldn't mind having them as in-laws."

"Mom! Stop it! I haven't even had a date with him yet."

"I'm telling Morgan," said Mac. "He needs to know Mom has prequalified him. He can get on with the wedding plans now."

Remy tried to cripple her brother with a well-placed kick, but Dad grabbed her to stop a full-scale fight. "Rafe is going to run, did you hear?" he said. "I might work on his campaign. I haven't felt good about a candidate in years."

"If Mr. Campbell wins," Mac pointed out, "Morgan'll move."

That was a year off. Remy had tomorrow to think of first.

Concert-choir fantasy aside, what would Morgan

57

say to her in school? Tomorrow was Friday. A very important fact. He'd want to go out this weekend, wouldn't he? After those kisses, wouldn't he want to see her right away? He couldn't stand it, could he?

Mac interpreted every expression on her face. "I have several hundred important calls to make," he said. "The phone will never be free."

Morgan avoided his family easily. Each of them had a private phone line, and they were all on the phone.

When I take my sign, thought Morgan, I'll keep it in the basement.

He went down to the basement where he kept his free weights. He peeled off his shirt and cords and got right to work, getting rid of the screaming energy collected in his muscles.

Only Morgan ever went into the basement. His parents were not basement people. They did not fix things; they paid others to do that. They didn't know where their fuse box was, or how the furnace ran, or where the shutoff valves were. Dad owned few tools and kept those in the garage. Mom had bought this house partly because each bedroom had its own bath with washer-dryer. No laundry room at all, let alone one in the basement.

He worked out, then moved over to the rowing machine, until sweat ran satisfyingly down his body.

Thank God for weights.

Morgan never argued. His sister, Starr, now, she was a champion arguer. But Morgan could never think of anything to say. He always just wanted to leave the room.

The thought was not a mild *Maybe I'll leave the room.* It was seething, roiling energy that began in his legs, demanding laps around a track. Words did not form. Speech did not come. Instead every muscle in his body kicked in, shouting for exercise. When other people could argue, Morgan needed to hit punching bags.

It had been a great night. There had been no real danger in his life for a long time. He wanted more of it.

He laughed at himself. Like taking a sign equals danger, he thought ruefully.

He picked up his clothes from the cellar floor, went up two flights, and stuffed them in his washing machine. He had so much crammed in there now there wasn't room for water. The sleeve of his sweater wouldn't go in.

He wondered what it would be like under Remy's sweater.

By morning Remy was rehearsed for anything.

She was prepared to be ignored totally, in case Morgan had changed his mind or never had his mind the way she wanted it. In case Morgan was wholly involved with Chase and Taft on some dumb subject like pro football and never looked her way.

If that happened, she had to get through it without a change of expression, never mind desperate sobbing or crazed pleading.

On the other hand, she was ready to be asked out in front of the whole class. To be kissed and hugged in public.

If that happened she also had to act normal. Like of course this was usual for her.

She ran her mind over the schedule of the day, and that portion she shared with Morgan Campbell.

Driver's Ed . . . Mr. Fielding could not possibly take the same three kids driving three days in a row.

Even Mr. Fielding would notice a certain repetition among faces. So she and Morgan would stay in the library.

Would they acknowledge each other? Would they allow the world to catch a glimpse of what had passed between them last night? Would they allow themselves to admit it?

Morgan Campbell woke up in the morning feeling like a rag doll with button eyes. Never mind weight lifting and rowing. He had to handle having a crush on a girl, and he had to do it in front of people. The whole idea made him limp.

In Concert Choir, Morgan's eyes were so stuck to the music page, there might have been magnets involved.

In Driver's Ed he walked blindly next to Chase, and hid behind Taft, like a toddler behind his mother.

He didn't look Remy's way. He didn't talk to her. He didn't wave.

He was so practiced at ignoring his parents and staying silent next to them that it was relatively easy to ignore Remy and stay silent next to her. How will she know I want to do it again, he thought, if I ignore her?

He went on ignoring her. Actually, *ignore* was hardly the word. Except for Remy, Morgan was hardly even conscious. She was the world, and yet there he was focusing on ceiling cracks and linoleum splits.

Error, he thought, the word flickering in his mind the way it did on computer screens.

This was a game of chicken in which he was the chicken, and if he didn't get brave, he'd be a loser forever.

He didn't get brave. He just tightened in on himself, as if he were a fortress in need of defense.

He skipped Current Events. The stress of another class with Remy was too much.

JV games began at four-thirty.

Girls of Remy's grade and playing level had usually given up by now. Remy didn't have good hands, or a feel for movement and strategy. She often wondered why she stuck with basketball. But sitting on the bench, toes pressed down hard inside her thick sneakers, she would yearn to play. You never knew whether the coach would put you in. His rotations were based on something Remy did not understand and which the parents said grumpily was called favoritism.

It was clear that Morgan Campbell was sorry he had ever gotten near her. By the light of day he must have realized Remy did not possess the perfection he required. Morgan was probably even now fantasizing about Alexandra.

Remy wanted to go home and cry; cry for hours; cry for years.

She was stuck with the basketball schedule and must play against Central. She made herself think of other things. Socks. Who yanked them up and who scrunched them down. Hair. Whose fell out of the ponytail and whose bangs were sweaty wet.

"Remy!" bellowed the coach. "Pay attention! This is *basket*ball!" As if she had been playing soccer.

A teacher paused carelessly in the door, his timing stating clearly that JV games were worth no more.

Remy's father, loaded down with videocam and baby brother, and her mother, burdened with diapers, snack, bottle, toys, juice, and blanket, trooped in. Mom shouted hello to other parents, kissed little brothers and sisters, greeted older brothers and sisters, noticed who had grown and who'd had haircuts and who was wearing new shoes.

"Remy! This is *basket*ball!"

Remy forced herself back into the game.

Morgan and Lark walked into the gym and climbed the bleachers to the top.

Morgan, like any boy, never had been, never would be, at a girls' JV game. Morgan, however, was at a girls' JV game.

Right away there was a call against Remy.

"Are you blind?" her father screamed. His hobby was Helping the Ref. In the first quarter he still had a clean mouth. "What are you, a shoe salesman? You got two eyes?"

Remy's teammates looked at her long and sadly. Their fathers had clean mouths. Their fathers did not embarrass the entire team and school. Their fathers sat next to Remy's, though, and egged him on.

If Remy's team was ahead, Dad was sometimes able to remain calm. If they were getting shellacked, Dad would kick the bleachers and shout things about the ref's family background. Frequently Dad informed the ref that his brain was located in another part of his body.

Not in front of Morgan, Remy prayed. Come on, God, do your thing. Keep Dad's mouth shut. Let me make a basket. Let Morgan be here with Lark because Morgan arranged it, not because Lark did.

Lark and Morgan sat beneath a huge banner made by the cheerleaders, proclaiming, WE WILL CRUSH YOU!

Lark was happy. She had been asked, she knew, in the role of escort, to make it possible for Morgan to attend. If he came alone he would be obvious, but if he wandered in with Remy's girlfriend Lark, nobody would think anything of it. It was important, when you were getting interested in a girl, that nobody should be able to tell.

Of course, every girl could always tell, but the boys thought they were being crafty and invisible.

Mr. Marland whistled with two fingers in his mouth. He sounded like a freight train ripping through the building.

Lark did not know how her parents would behave in public. They never came to anything, even teacher conferences. They had basically skipped Lark's life. She didn't mind. She had made her own.

And her own game involved looking out for herself, since nobody else was doing it. Nickie Budie's voice, when he'd called Thursday afternoon to arrange a pickup time, had been a warning signal. He was a Future Criminal of America if there ever was one, and what had seemed like an amusing adventure suddenly sounded tricky. THICKLY SETTLED was nice, but not getting caught was nicer.

Lark hoped Remy would play well in front of Morgan, although Remy didn't play well in front of anybody else, so why would she rise to this occasion? Rumor had it once the season started, Remy wouldn't be kept on Junior Varsity, a form of humiliation few suffered.

Lark herself competed only in sports without spectators. Never in this world would Lark be a fool in front of a crowd. Field hockey and softball were okay because nobody ever came. Basketball was different. By the third quarter, and definitely the fourth, the gym would begin to fill. People arriving for Varsity would want to see how the younger girls were doing; what their potential was.

She glanced at Morgan. Yes, definitely a boy deciding what the potential was.

"Blue ball!" the ref shouted.

"A blind man can see it's White!" bellowed Mr. Marland.

Morgan loved the Marlands. They were so obvious. What you saw was what you got. You could see Mrs. Marland across a gym and know that her first name was Imogene and she was receptionist in a pediatric practice. You could listen to Mr. Marland and know that he would always believe in his daughter's abilities, whether she had any or not.

Plus, whenever you watched the Marlands, you were always glad you had different parents.

Remy was fouled. One and one.

Morgan prayed for her. Let her make them both!

She sank the first one.

In games you could always yell for the player. So Morgan was free to yell, and he yelled, "Way to go, Remy!"

She bounced the ball four times, trying to drain off tension.

I'll ask her out after the game, he thought. I'll tell her I was an idiot for not talking to her during class.

He knew he would do neither one.

Okay, then, I'll call her tonight, he thought.

That was far enough off that he could believe he might really do it.

* * *

64

Morgan was not in the gym when Remy and her team got out of the locker room. Morgan was not at Pizza Hut to celebrate the JV victory. Morgan had left no messages with Lark. And that night, though Remy waited and circled and prayed, the phone did not ring.

What was the point in having a God if he did not make the phone ring when you wanted it to?

Friday night, and the phone was not ringing. She had a sick glance down the hallways of her life; a horror that all of her Friday nights would be phoneless.

No, God, she said forcefully. Anything but that.

Saturday would come and go, filled with the chores of a working family: groceries, laundry, vacuuming, a rented movie to fill the evening.

Sunday would arrive and here she was, irked with God. Why could the Marlands never skip church like normal people?

When she was little, Remy loved church.

It was so mysterious. Why had everybody come? Why were they dressed up? Why did they serve such strange food? Why did you pay for this, hiding your money in little white envelopes?

By her teens, however, Remy detested church. It was not mysterious. It was dumb. Everybody was a hypocrite. There was no point and when she had children of her own she would not subject them to this. Her kids would play on soccer teams with Sunday-morning games. So there.

Thinking of Mrs. Willit's awful sermons made her think of Mr. Willit, nominating Morgan for normalcy.

If Morgan were normal, she thought, he would have stayed after the game and asked me out.

"Let's quit going to church," Remy said to her brother. "Will you quit with me?"

65

Mac could not stand being on his sister's side, so even if he detested church ninety times more than Remy, which he did, he couldn't agree with her. "Of course not," he said. "Do you think I want to hurt Mom?" He continued to drink out of the orange juice carton, letting it dribble down his chin and spill on the floor where Remy would step in it.

She was sick of this. She wanted to make a dent in the world. If Morgan Campbell wouldn't call, something else would have to happen.

Like a watchman in a city of old, Morgan's mother called out, "Eleven o'clock approaching!" In some families the warning meant bedtime. In Morgan Campbell's it meant the late news.

Rafe and Nance Campbell and their son and daughter gathered before the televisions.

Dad channel-grazed, remoting at high speed from station to station. Stalking lions on PBS blended into diamond rings on Home Shopper, evaporating into wrestling matches on ESPN, only to dissolve into rock stars on MTV.

"This is the kind of dangerous light pattern that sets off convulsions in small children, Daddy," said Starr.

Dad grinned and stopped. He left the sound on for the local ABC news affiliate, their usual favorite.

Morgan liked the late-night commentators. He knew them as well as any family friend.

Anne was slender, graceful, and utterly lovely.

Rob was thick, stern, and heavy lidded.

Sports were handled by Chuck, who grinned steadily; he knew he had the best job on earth.

Weather was Irene, a confused middle-aged woman who worried so much about the possibility of snow that

66

Morgan assumed she had no life, but spent her existence staring at weather patterns and feeling desperate.

"And now a new dimension to vandalism in our city," said Anne, smoothing her papers and looking kind and sweet. Anne's hair was neither blond nor gray, but truly silver, as if she had come off a starship. "The smashing of mailboxes is well known to us; there have been five sieges of this destruction since the opening of city schools on September second."

Starr moaned. "Tell us how kids today are responsible for everything," she said to Anne.

Eleven-ten, thought Morgan. Too late to call Remy now. The weekend is shot. And now Remy'll be mad at me and by Monday she'll hate me.

He tried to reconstruct the feeling of her lips and hair, but he seemed to have no touch memory. To know it again he would have to do it again.

His mouth was dry.

"And now, a spate of sign stealing has hit the suburban areas, with terrible results." Anne looked gravely into Morgan's eyes.

Sign stealing.

What terrible results? That sounded like media hype to Morgan. How could there be terrible results from taking a street name?

He was not nervous, exactly. He was a plane that was not landing. Waiting for permission to come down. Holding-pattern tense.

"Last night," said Anne, "a fatal car accident occurred at the corner of Warren Street and Cherry Road."

His mother passed a wicker basket filled with skinny stick pretzels. Starr made pretzel-stick people on the coffee table.

The camera panned over the intersection Morgan had left twenty-four hours before. His mouth got drier and then his eyes dried, too, as if he were evaporating.

"A car driven by twenty-six-year-old Denise Thompson was hit broadside by a truck. Denise Thompson was killed instantly. Police say this is a particularly dangerous intersection. There is supposed to be a stop sign on Cherry Road. But when Mrs. Thompson, driving home after dropping her baby-sitter off, came to the intersection with Warren Street, there was no stop sign."

The camera slipped slowly over a blue car so completely crushed by a mason's dump truck that Morgan could not tell if it was a sedan or a wagon, old or new, American or foreign. The front door had been cut off to extricate the driver. The opening bore no resemblance to a door's shape. It was a twisted cave.

"Today, police tried to reconstruct the incident," said Anne, and now on television, the wrecked car was gone. Towed away. Traffic flowed on Warren. Life—except Denise Thompson's—went on.

Morgan was screaming on the inside. It was soundless, yet so loud that jet engines might have been taking off in his brain. *There is supposed to be a stop sign on Cherry Road.*

A reporter on the scene addressed a policeman. "Do you have any idea who did this?"

"Kids," said the cop, shrugging. He had seen it before, he would see it again. "They don't think. They like the shape of stop signs, you know. We hafta replace 'em all the time. Kids probably figure whoever's driving here will figure it out. You know, stop whether the sign's there or not. Kids don't stop to think. They forget that eventually it's the middle of the night. No traffic. No clues. This Denise Thompson, she's a stranger to the road, she needs that stop sign."

The stop sign that stood on its side in Morgan's garage.

His veins and arteries were expanding as if he were going to explode.

"When do you think the sign was taken?" asked the reporter.

"Neighbor said it was here when she got home from shopping around nine," said the cop. "Accident happened ten-eighteen. Cut on the posts is fresh, you can see the contrast right here." The camera zeroed in. The slice that Morgan had made with Nickie's hacksaw glittered clean and metallic at the top of the grimy posts.

No, thought Morgan. That didn't happen. It was just a sign. We weren't doing anything. *It was just a sign.*

A weeping man, face so distorted by pain it was impossible to tell what he really looked like, swatted away the microphone. Even so, it picked up his screams. "My wife is dead!" he shouted. "We have a two-year-old! He's lost his mother! All because some goddamn kid thought it was fun to take a stop sign."

Some goddamn kid.

Morgan's mind burned. His heart seemed to catch fire. He was so hot and dry, he felt blistered. He wanted to look at his skin but could not take his eyes off the screen.

Nobody died, he thought. Not because of me. I'm a nice person. It was only a sign.

The husband was opening his wallet, ripping it apart, throwing useless things like credit cards and twenty-dollar bills to the ground. He yanked out a photograph and held it up to the camera. His hand was shaking. The reporter steadied the picture for his crew.

A pretty young woman, brown hair falling into her eyes, was stretching her hands out to a tottering child. Her smile was complete; you knew that at that moment, her world had been complete too: full of love and rejoicing and a perfect healthy baby.

"Denise Thompson," said Anne, "leaves her husband, Mark, and a two-year-old son, Bobby."

No.

"Anybody with information about this act of vandalism, which led to an innocent woman's death," said Anne invisibly, "should telephone police at the phone number seen on your screen."

Denise Thompson's husband looked both wild and helpless. Out of control, yet too weak to move. Suddenly he wanted the microphone, and he seized it, paying no attention to reporter or cameraman.

"If I find the kid that took that sign . . ."

He wiped his eyes with the hand that held the mike. ". . . If I find out who murdered my wife . . . who left our son without his mother . . ."

Mark Thompson did not finish his threat. He stared past the cameras and into his future. He seemed to fold, and become smaller. After a while he let go of the mike and stumbled away.

The camera followed him silently.

The police phone number stayed on the screen.

The number seemed to memorize itself; began playing in his head like lyrics to a song. Morgan looked away from the television, but of course the room was full of televisions: three more of them, their blank gray

70

screens like coffins. If he turned them on, they, too, would speak of stolen signs and dead mothers.

It was just a sign! he thought. Everybody does it. It doesn't count. It's—

"Whoever took that sign," said Rafe Campbell, "should be shot."

CHAPTER 5

"Mac," said Remy, "you just told Daddy that was de-caf."

Mac grinned. "So he won't sleep well tonight."

"Mac! Daddy believed you. He had two cups."

Remy's brother laughed contentedly to himself.

"Mother, does anybody need a person like Mac? Don't you think Mac should be in boarding school?"

"Yes."

"Then why isn't he?"

"We can't afford it. Otherwise we would have shipped him away years ago."

Mac loved this kind of talk.

"What if the baby turns out like Mac?" said Remy.

"Don't worry about it," said Mac. "You're fifteen years older than he is. You'll never know how Matthew turns out. By the time Matthew's in second grade, you'll have your own baby."

This was thought provoking, but not enough to take her mind off Morgan. He wouldn't telephone this late. She might as well give up. At least she hadn't confided in Lark. She could keep her ruined hopes in her heart, instead of lying around for Lark to laugh at and pick on.

Being a Marland, Remy consoled herself with a final dose of junk food before bed. She ate the other half of her Heath bar, while Mom had another chocolate-covered doughnut, and Mac, an immense helping of pineapple ice cream. Mac preferred flavors nobody else would touch, thus ensuring there was always enough for him.

The phone rang.

Morgan's been sitting by the phone trying to work up courage! Remy thought joyfully. He forgot the time, but who cares? The thing is to get Mac away from me so I can hold a real conversation.

Naturally at this hour, Mom thought somebody was dead or in a dreadful accident, and she leaped across the food line to the phone. "Lark?" said Mom in astonishment. "Do you have any idea what time it is?"

Lark? thought Remy. She must be checking to see if Morgan called. I'll lie. No, I'll tell the truth. No, I don't want to lie or tell the truth. I'll tell her I can't talk.

"Is this important, Lark?" said Mom severely. "Can this wait until morning?"

"Come on, Mom," said Mac. "We're not doing anything earth shattering here. We're just chewing. On a Friday night. Let Remy talk."

Mac on her team? That in itself was earth shattering. Remy took the phone.

"Don't talk where they can hear you," whispered Lark.

"Huh?"

"Did you see the news?" Lark's voice was abnormally husky.

73

"Me? No. What news?" Unless it was war or her favorite department store leaving the mall, Remy wouldn't be interested. The Marlands were not news minded. They took a local paper, mostly for sports. Remy herself read the comics, Ann Landers, her horoscope, and the ads. Rarely did the Marlands glance at television news.

"Don't talk out loud, Remy!" hissed Lark.

Remy giggled. "What other way to talk is there?"

"Remy, listen to me." Lark sounded strained and peculiar.

There *is* a war, thought Remy. Which of the many countries they followed in Current Events had finally gone over the edge and drawn the United States in? She considered the senior boys that Lark adored and wondered if they, thrilled by this violent turn of events, were running to a recruitment office to enlist.

"A woman got killed last night," said Lark. "It was just on the news. Somebody took a stop sign. She drove through an intersection and got pasted by a truck."

"Oh," said Remy. "How sad."

"Remy. Are you listening to me?"

Remy was not. Not really. She was rehearsing how to share everything about Morgan and yet keep the best parts secret in her heart. She was—

—*took a stop sign.*

"The police said teenagers probably stole the stop sign," said Lark.

Remy was listening.

"The husband was on TV," said Lark. "They had a police information number on the screen."

"She died?" whispered Remy.

"She died," said Lark.

74

"What was the corner?" said Remy. But she knew. She knew right down into her bones, as if she were the dead person.

Remy Marland had just made a dent in the world.

The late-night news went on.

Rafe Campbell sipped his white wine and Nance Campbell indulged in two more skinny pretzel sticks.

Anne discussed the economy, which was worse. Irene was distraught over the possibility of precipitation. Chuck could hardly wait for his turn and the details of a locker-room fracas.

"By the way, Morgan, I want to wear the red velvet cape with the ermine trim," said Starr. "And the biggest crown."

Morgan had no idea what his sister was talking about.

"Mom, make him give me the best king costume."

"Why would Morgan make that decision?"

"He's going to run the Christmas pageant."

"Morgan, darling, how wonderful!" exclaimed his mother. "I'm so proud. You'll do such a lovely job. I adore the pageant."

Do they let killers run Christmas pageants? thought Morgan. The thing is not to think about it. If I think about it, somebody might see it in my eyes. Be able to tell what I did. So I won't think about it.

Starr was the blackmailer of the century.

I am not thinking about the stop sign, he thought, and faced her. His hands had gotten thick; the swelling was noticeable. If he'd been wearing his class ring, it would have hurt. Did guilt puff you up?

"I'm your sister," said Starr, "and that means I get first dibs on costumes."

"Will you let the Marland baby be Jesus again this year?" said Mom.

A woman who pretends her kid is Jesus, thought Morgan. What happens when she finds out her other kid helped kill somebody?

He had known the truth for five minutes. Already he was trying to spread the blame. Remy had never gone near the stop sign. Even Nickie—all he'd done was to choose it. But Nickie was a weakling. Morgan was the only one who had actually used the hacksaw.

"Can't you wait for the ads to talk?" said Dad. Even though it was only weather, he hated distractions when he was receiving information.

Mom, however, talked when she felt like it. "I recommend against it," said Mom. "He's a toddler now. You can't predict what a one-year-old will do. He might scream or run away or throw up."

"Neat," said Starr. "Jesus the vomiter."

"Leave the room if you have to babble!" shouted Dad.

Whoever did that should be shot.

Dad would shoot me. But he doesn't know. But he could. Easily. The signs are in the garage! I have to get rid of them.

What if Dad caught him?

His father was a big voice for Law and Order. Would he stick with that? Would Morgan go to prison? Or would he and his father destroy the evidence? Just a little father-son activity on a rainy weekend.

That's right, he thought, think about yourself. A woman is dead, her little kid doesn't have a mother. But don't think about that. Hey. Put yourself first.

He took his father's advice and left the room. He made it upstairs. He didn't fall down or scream or put his fist through the wall or anything. He shut the door neatly behind him.

They were very privacy minded, the Campbells. Nobody would dream of coming in anybody else's room without permission. They met only in the kitchen, in front of the television, or inside the car.

I'm safe in here, thought Morgan.

And Denise Thompson. She was safe where she was too.

Safe in a drawer at the morgue.

Remy did not sleep.

It was an event that had never happened in her sixteen years. Total insomnia. Her eyes never seemed to blink, let alone close. She lay in the dark thinking: Don't let it be ruined. Don't let Morgan hate me for being there. For seeing him. For saying yes to the whole thing. I want to have Morgan still!

Nice, Remy.

You kill a woman and all you're worried about is whether Morgan kisses you again.

If Mom finds out . . .

So tell her first. Face the music.

But it would not be music. It was not music you faced when you killed somebody.

What did you face? Remy did not know.

How could it be me? I don't do bad things. I don't think bad things or say bad things. I can't be part of this!

She tilted the ankle and the foot that had such fun driving. She imagined Denise Thompson's foot on the gas pedal as she followed Cherry Road; Denise Thompson's confusion as she found herself in the middle of— *a truck—where did ? that ? come from?—rip foot off gas*

77

—slam brake—slew to the side—try to avoid—try!—no!
—too late—too—

But Remy could follow Denise Thompson no further.

Midnight passed and Friday turned into Saturday.

No school in the morning; no world to face. He who had not even been able to face guesses about his crush on Remy. How would he face Driver's Ed, where everybody had talked about taking signs? How would he face Lark, who knew which three had gone out sign-stealing when? How would he face Remy, who had been there?

In Current Events, Morgan had been astonished to find half the kids never watched the news. He'd assumed the entire world curled up in front of the TV each night to see what had happened in the last twenty-four hours. But no. Plenty of people couldn't care less. It was entirely possible that Remy did not know about Denise Thompson.

Nickie would almost certainly not know. He had his own television and watched exclusively MTV, cartoons, and sports.

Lark couldn't actually know. But she could make a very good guess.

And the class.

They couldn't know.

But they could guess.

Who had watched that broadcast?

Who had written down the police number?

Who was deciding whether to call? Christine, who thought it was wrong? Would she tell?

The odds, Morgan told himself, are that everybody was at the movies, or a party, or playing Nintendo. If they were watching TV, it was a talk show, not the news. If they watched the news, it was some other channel. Besides, a car accident. Happens all the time. People probably got up and got another piece of cake while Anne spent time over yet another traffic incident.

Incident.

A woman is dead, thought Morgan, and I who killed her am trying to call that an "incident."

Dawn was sluggish and reluctant, the death of night instead of the birth of day. Remy left her bed, and stood barefoot and shivering in front of the window. Trees in the yard were thin and brittle without leaves. Already their autumn color had vanished, and only the deadness of coming winter remained.

It was just a sign, Remy said to herself.

Just a piece of wood on a post. That woman was probably a lousy driver anyhow. Maybe the road was slick. Maybe she was reaching down to the floor to get her coffee cup where she'd wedged it. Maybe she was singing along to the radio and not paying attention to the road anyhow. Maybe it was her own fault.

Saturday passed.

Remy stayed home with Henry while everybody else was out doing interesting things. Sometime in the middle of the afternoon, when they were crawling backward down the stairs, which was his new thrill of the week, she thought: Denise Thompson's little boy isn't much older than this.

She isn't crawling backward down the stairs with her baby son. She's dead. She'll never see her little boy grow up.

Remy began sobbing, first soundlessly and then with

huge bawling groans. She actually felt better from it, and cried more, and the hot acidic tears seemed to drain off some of the horror.

Her little brother was stunned. He was the one who cried. Not his big sister! His world split open and he clung to Remy. His tiny clumsy hands patted her cheeks. "Me?" he said frantically. "Me?"

It's his first word, she thought, and it's not *me*, it's *Remy*. He's saying my name.

Bobby Thompson would be calling his Mommy today, trying to find her, looking for her in her usual places, raising his voice. Mommy. Where are you? Mommy would never answer.

Oh, God! thought Remy. Why weren't you there? Why didn't you make me stop? Why didn't you make Denise Thompson stop?

His first word had gotten him nowhere. Her little brother began screaming with her, the center of his world caving in, until he didn't even want Remy to hold him anymore, because it was too scary.

Saturday passed.

The accident was not on the news again. It was old already. Now Anne of the silver hair was distressed because a football coach had been caught selling drugs and a young housewife had masterminded a mail scam.

Saturday had one use. Morgan had time to move THICKLY SETTLED and STOP to his cellar. He thought the signs would disappear into the dim corners, but they did not. They shouted their color and size and words even with their backs turned.

Sunday they went to church, as Starr had predicted.

Morgan, who considered Not Listening to Sermons one of his more polished skills, listened. Hoping for clues. Wanting Mrs. Willit to give him—what? An excuse? A way out?

"There's an interesting passage in the New Testament," said Mrs. Willit. She was given to fatuous remarks. Morgan would never know why Mr. Willit stayed with her. In this era of divorce it often seemed the wrong marriages lasted.

"Jesus hasn't begun his ministry yet. He's still living at home. Hasn't done a thing. Hasn't told a parable, hasn't got a single follower, hasn't pulled off any miracles. He gets baptized in the River Jordan and from the heavens comes the voice of God."

Morgan detested this kind of story. Nobody heard the voice of God, except schizophrenics in padded rooms.

"And God says, '*This is my beloved son, in whom I am well pleased.*'"

Come on, thought Morgan. How pleased can you be with a thirty-year-old son who hasn't held a job yet?

"God is pleased even before His Son has done anything. His Son has no accomplishments, and still, God is pleased."

Morgan was sitting between his parents. His beautiful mother, wearing her long black cashmere coat, was on his right. His brilliant father, in charcoal gray, perfect tie, perfect crease, was on his left. They were one up on God. Their son and daughter had already been impressive. By age thirty Morgan and Starr would have done a lot more than a little carpentry in some backwater village. Jesus could get away with that, but not Starr and Morgan.

His father spindled the Sunday bulletin and then flattened it out and made a paper airplane. Mom laid a stern hand on the airplane, even though Dad was the least likely person in the church actually to fly it. They gave each other secret grins. People-in-love-in-spite-of-everything grins.

"Unconditional love. That's what parents give their children," said Mrs. Willit.

But surely every parent had some conditions. Like: I will love you as long as you're not a murderer.

Whoever took that sign should be shot.

Oh, Dad! thought Morgan, and he actually splinted himself against the pain in his soul, bending at the waist.

Remy and Morgan had been in Sunday school together for years. Their Sunday school was deeply into arts and crafts, so they'd turned out cotton-ball Christmas sheep, folded-box Noah's arks, and vividly colored Joseph's coats. Together they had memorized commandments, received attendance ribbons, and sung in Junior Choir.

In eighth grade, just when boys ought to start thinking how much they liked this girl they knew so well, the Campbells had faded, to be seen only on holidays.

This was sensible, because church was best on holidays. At Christmas you were starry eyed and believed in babies without birth defects, presents with perfect ribbons, and snow without pollution. Remy approved of the Campbells coming only on holidays.

But here they were on a dull ordinary November Sunday, not even Thanksgiving.

Morgan told, she thought. He told, and they're here to ask God's help. Tell Mrs. Willit, because she's the minister. Then she'll tell Mr. Willit, who thinks I'm nice, and in a minute the world will know.

Suddenly Concert Choir seemed like the most important forty-five minutes of any day, with Mr. Willit laughing and teasing and leading and loving. He would never look her way again; he would write her off, one of the dirtbags. Because nobody played favorites as much as Mr. Willit, not even the basketball coach. *I don't want him to know*, she prayed.

Dad was laughing in Mr. Campbell's direction. "Guess he's running," said Remy's father under his breath.

"Those are definitely campaign-speech clothes," agreed Remy's mother.

Morgan didn't tell, thought Remy. It's just a campaign thing.

Relief went through her like thick medicine.

Coffee hour actually lasted twenty minutes. Kids loved it. There was always an immense sheet cake with thick Crisco and confectioners' sugar icing, plus hundreds of doughnut holes and cups of apple juice.

Morgan loved icing. It was kind of nice to be back at coffee hour, where he hadn't wasted time in years. He cut himself a corner, swept off the icing with two fingers, and tossed the cake part away. He started to eat the icing and smashed car filled his mouth instead, destroyed flesh, broken bones, spilled brains.

With difficulty he reached a pile of napkins. He could not separate them.

Rafe and Nance were shaking hands all over the place, laughing, nodding, agreeing, admitting. "Yes, he's going to run," said Morgan's mother. "Isn't it exciting? The actual announcement won't come until spring. I know we can count on you to work with us." She made the campaign sound like a year-long party. People adored Nance, even when she whipped out her ever-present notebook to take names.

Morgan managed to get the icing off his fingers. He was an exhibit of sickness: his complexion had changed, his breathing was different, his eyelid was trembling.

One of the feminists of the church descended on Nance to demand why Nance wasn't running instead of her husband.

Morgan meant to listen for the answer, because he had often wondered himself, but Mac came up, smirking as if he and Morgan shared a secret.

There was only one secret.

He knows, thought Morgan. Remy told him. Or Mac found her Morgan Road sign. And made her tell. *This worthless little cowpat knows what we did.*

What would happen? What would his father do to him? What would the law do to him? What about college?

Remy, pink-cheeked and golden-haired, was wearing a dress, which was unusual for her even on Sunday. It was a lovely loose dress, in soft colors with soft folds. If they went on a date, he would want her to wear that, not utility wear, like jeans.

He was swamped by romantic thoughts, images that had never before entered his mind: getting her flowers, buying her presents. "Hi, Remy," he said awkwardly. "How are you?"

Her paper cake-plate fluttered in her hand. He wanted to help her eat the cake, hold the plate for her, smooth life for her.

Oh, yeah, like I could smooth anybody's life, he thought. Look how well I did smoothing Denise Thompson's life.

"Guess what?" said worthless little Mac, grinning evilly at Morgan.

Morgan tried to stay steady. It came to him that he, Morgan, was the worthless one now. Nobody but Mac knew yet. *Oh, God.* I have to tell my parents before Mac does. We have to get out of here, so I can—

"You'll be glad to know my mother has prequalified you for marriage," said Mac.

"Huh?"

"Remy has a crush on you," said Mac. "So does my Mom." Mac whapped his sister's wrist so her cake flew off the plate and icing spattered all over the floor.

"Lick it up," Morgan told him.

Mac immediately fell to his knees and began licking the sugary linoleum.

Remy said, "I of course will adopt rather than have children of my own. No need to touch the Marland family genes."

She doesn't know, he thought. If she knew, she couldn't joke. So what do I do? Tell her myself? Hope it all goes away?

He wondered if that was actually a possibility. That it could all go away.

"What are you two so intent on?" demanded Starr, wedging in.

Like he was going to tell Starr anything. "The pageant," said Morgan. He hurried to dig up Mrs. Willit.

What's the matter with me? he thought. Death doesn't all go away. I might not get caught with the stop sign, but Denise Thompson will always be caught dead.

People said Nickie Budie was pond scum. Nobody had ever said it of Morgan Campbell. But it was true now. Morgan had just turned into the definition of

85

scum: one who forgot the dead woman and thought only of getting away with it.

In what sounded like a perfectly normal voice, he informed Mrs. Willit that he wanted to run the pageant this year.

Mrs. Willit was overly thrilled. "Ooooh, it's so difficult to find people to do that," she cried. "The pageant is such a nuisance really. I'd skip it, but people don't think it's Christmas without a pageant. Nance, you have such fine children. I mean, really. What a splendid dear dear boy." Mrs. Willit hugged him. Morgan remained calm, only because he could see his father being hugged by someone equally unfortunate, and handling it fine.

"I get to be a king," said Starr, shoving up against her brother.

Everybody laughed. People patted Starr's hair, as if she were a sweet little thing, instead of the meanest kid in junior high.

I'm a splendid dear dear boy, Morgan told himself. Even if it came from Mrs. Willit, it's true. I'm a nice person. *I have not killed anybody.* It was just a sign.

CHAPTER 6

Monday came, as Mondays do. Relentlessly.

It was a beautiful morning, surprisingly warm for so late in the fall. A morning on which nobody could be dead. But Denise Thompson was.

Remy had looked in the newspaper, unusual for her, and read the obituary. The funeral had been Sunday afternoon. Denise Thompson was underground.

"Come on," said Mom. "I can*not* be late for work. Move it."

Remy strapped the baby into his car seat. He was still eating his toast, which occupied him too much to fight the seat belt. Henry's kiss smeared her cheek with butter and jam and for some reason she didn't want to wipe it off; she wanted to take it to school with her, a shiny little mark of love.

Mom backed fast out of the drive. Remy couldn't begin to back up that smoothly. She glanced for traffic, training herself, and saw that every single mailbox on their road had been smashed.

"The third time in two weeks!" yelled Mac. When Mom stopped at the bottom of the drive, he opened his door, as if to vault out and find a clue at the base of the splintered post. "I'm gonna sue 'em! Why, those little—"

Mom cut off Mac's favorite noun. "Don't say it. Just get back in the car, Mac. Once Remy gets her license, you'll have another forty-five minutes every morning, but not today."

I don't want a license now. I don't want to drive. Once it was funny, going over a cement divider. No big deal, we said. Nobody died. *But somebody died.*

Mac went on and on about the mailboxes. "I have to dig out the stupid hole! Buy another post! Sink it in cement!" He'd have played mailbox baseball, too, if he'd had friends with cars. But since it was his job to replace the box, the hobby was less attractive.

How could she fake it through Driver's Ed? Morgan had trembled in church, as if she were a threat. She had babbled her way through coffee hour. Could she babble her way through school? Should she pretend to be sick and stay home?

But skipping school would be an admission.

I have to act normal. I can't let them pick up on anything. It has to stay a secret. I cannot let anybody think I'm the kind of person who does things like that.

"Forty-three," said Mom grimly.

"Forty-three what?" said Mac.

"Mailboxes. I could sit up with a shotgun and nail those worthless little delinquents."

Even Mac took a second look at their mother. Mom actually sounded as if she would empty a shotgun into teenagers playing mailbox baseball. Remy had the nightmarish sense of somebody pouring water down her throat without letting her swallow; filling her up; drowning her. If Mom hated somebody who hit pieces

of metal that much, how much would she hate somebody who . . .

Remy grabbed her own hair. Literally holding herself together.

Forget Mr. Willit. It's Mom who can't know! Mom
would kill me. Or herself.

The baby blew bubbles. This was his great artistic
achievement—covering his tiny chin with saliva, giggling softly while the bubbles slid down and kept his
chest wet all day. He admired the way his sister held her
hand on her head, and he worked at putting his hand
on his head. He accomplished it and beamed at Remy.

"Listen to the rumors in school, Mac," said Mom.
"Find out who it is. I'm going to get hold of their parents. I just know they come from the kind of family
where the mother and father don't even care what their
children are doing."

"Wait a minute," protested Mac. "What rumors am
I going to hear? Eighth graders don't drive. Remy's
grade plays mailbox baseball. Remy'll hear the rumors."

"Your sister does not hang out with the sort of creep
who would do that," said their mother, as if she had the
slightest idea who was around Remy all day.

Mac opened his mouth to point this out, but they
had arrived at the day care, and it was his job to take
the baby in. Mac undid the seat belt and harness, kissing the only person to whom he showed affection.
"Come along, Matthew, my man," he said. He lifted his
little brother very carefully because diapers often
slipped and Mac didn't want to go to school with wet
hands.

Henry wrapped loving arms around Mac's neck,
reached under his brother's unzipped jacket, and tried

to take the Bic pens out of Mac's shirt pocket. Once this kid got his fingers wrapped around an object, you had to saw it free. Mac twisted hard to keep the pens safe.

"Bye, Sweet Prince," said Remy.

"Bye-bye, darling," said Mom to her baby. She kissed his little cheek when Mac held him down to her face, and murmured softly.

"What kind of person will he grow up to be with you two calling him Jesus or Sweet Prince?" shouted Mac. "Try to imagine junior high, will you?"

Remy would never willingly imagine junior high.

There was only one good thing about junior high: eventually it was replaced by senior high.

She prayed to the God of High Schools that he would turn her invisible for the day. Let nobody look at her, let no teacher call upon her.

Sometimes when she asked for things like this, she could feel warmth, as if her current god was listening, at least. Today there was nothing.

The fear of being found out puddled in her lungs.

School was simply school.

Accidents were not mentioned. Teachers taught. Homework was collected. Morgan didn't run into Nickie. Was Nickie home pretending to be sick? Would he lie low till it was over? How would they know when it was over?

At eleven o'clock Morgan walked carefully into the library, balancing himself, imitating his mother's wonderful smile and his father's cool. He smacked hands with Taft and Chase and opened a *Car and Driver* to memorize, just like always. He felt Remy's presence but did not look up.

Better nobody should realize she had gone along. Best if nobody realized Morgan had been there, either, but at least he could do his part to keep Remy safe. The thing was to pretend he had never known her.

Driver's Ed filled up. Was it his imagination, or were they all uncharacteristically quiet? Was he self-conscious, or were they all looking at corners or shoes, anywhere but at each other?

"Today," said Mr. Fielding, "nobody will go driving. A police officer is going to meet us out on the school lawn."

Police.

Morgan was immediately badly out of breath.

Shock, he thought. My lungs are closing down.

He tried to hide the quick, shallow breathing from Taft and Chase. Sequences of his life spun through Morgan's mind as if he were channel-grazing his future. Prison/handcuffs/trials. His father's horror blended into his mother turning away, his sister's cruel laugh.

"There was a terrible accident," said Mr. Fielding. "Did everybody hear about it?"

Accident. Morgan seized on the word. Yes. Totally accidental. Nothing to do with me.

Christine, assuming that not everybody had heard, repeated the television commentary. It was like a rerun from a younger, watered-down Anne. The words dripped in Morgan's ears like full sponges. He could wring his brain out.

"Why do they always blame kids?" said Kierstin, who got belligerent easily. She was duking up for a fight.

"And even if it is a kid," said Taft, "it'll be one of the scums who goes around keying cars and spray-painting buildings and breaking into vending machines. It won't be one of us." Taft looked to Morgan for confirmation.

Morgan could not stop himself from looking down at the tabletop and swallowing hard. When he looked up, Taft was staring at him.

"Everybody outside," said Mr. Fielding.

"It's cold out," said Lark, though it was not. "I have to get my coat." Lark would not join them on the lawn. She hated the outdoors and felt it had no right to exist.

The kids whined and complained. Why they were meeting this police officer on the lawn, instead of here in the classroom, nobody could imagine.

Morgan knew.

He was going to be arrested in front of his peers. They were going to make an example of him.

He pictured the phone call to his father. He hadn't talked to his father in years. The opening subjects would be jail and bail.

Somehow he stumbled with the rest out of the library and down the hall to the near exit. His feet landed on pavement and carried him across the bus drop-off circle.

He would not look at Remy. If he did, he would hang on to her, or she to him, and they would be ruined.

There, towed onto the winter-dying grass of the school campus, close to the flagpole, displayed to all traffic on Warren Street, was the vehicle that Denise Thompson had driven to her death.

It was so crumpled, so destroyed, Morgan did not know how they had gotten her corpse out. What parts of it had killed her? Remained stuck in her? Gone with her into the grave?

Kierstin and Cristin began to cry. Joss yanked out a little Kleenex pack and handed tissues around. No boy took one.

Morgan forced himself to look at the car. Taft was still watching him. Taft could not actually know, but he could guess. Morgan thought he had already guessed.

"So what've we got?" said the cop.

The steering wheel was folded in two, as if it had been made of Play-Doh.

"We've got a dead mother," said the cop.

Remy's sob escaped her throat, a high, awful keening, like a dying bird.

Don't do that! thought Morgan. You'll give us away.

But in the strange way of girls Cristin and Kierstin seemed to find Remy's reaction reasonable, and they comforted her.

"All because some teenager wanted a sign for his bedroom," said the cop. "You know what I mean? This woman died, she's not a whole lot older than you are, you know, and her baby's never gonna remember his mommy, all because some teenager didn't stop to think."

I was like Lark, Morgan thought. I stopped, but I didn't stay stopped.

"Probably the same kids that are playing mailbox baseball did this. Something to do. Thursday night, kids didn't care about their homework, just wanted something to do. Well, you just remember this," said the cop. "Denise Thompson is never going to have something to do again."

Wait.

The cop had not come to arrest him. This was just driver education. Just another lecture. The car was a visual aid. More impact than a film.

"How do you know it's kids?" demanded Kierstin. Police set her off. She saw a uniform or a blue light and she took the offense.

The cop knew her type, just as he knew the sign-stealing type. "Kids don't think."

"Some kids think," she argued.

She was boring him. He said, "I meet the ones who don't." The officer explained that it was state policy now to display car accidents rather than pretend they didn't happen. Therefore the wreck would lie on the lawn to sober the kids up. Speaking of sober, he added, the victim had been. Could have been plenty of alcohol in the vandals, though.

Christine coughed and fussed with her hair and her scarf. She looked like a person fidgeting with small decisions before making the big one. Christine, who had objected to the sign game.

Joss looked at Christine. Chase and Taft looked at Christine. Kierstin and Cristin looked at Christine. The eye pressure of peer pressure.

Morgan knew he should tell first. It would go better if he admitted it before they forced him to. I could leave Remy out, he thought. But would Nickie leave Remy out?

And the biggest *but* of all . . . would his father and mother go with him to the police station? He was no longer the kid they had in mind. The kid they had in mind did the right things.

The policeman got in his squad car.

The right thing would be to walk after the cop. Sir? May I talk to you for a minute?

Christine gave a funny little sigh and put a Kleenex to her eyes.

The cop started his engine and drove off with a sort of efficient speed, as if he could not get away from these kids and their sign-stealing fast enough.

Morgan replayed the night in Nickie's car. This time Good Morgan Campbell thought ahead to the consequences, because he was not a slime who keyed cars or spray-painted bridges.

But I am a slime. I'm glad I got away with it. I want to go on getting away with it.

He had a premonition of the headline: GOOD KID KILLS.

Kierstin poked Taft in the butt and got a nice reaction, equal parts irritated and flirty. Joss turned a cartwheel, whether to celebrate being alive when Denise Thompson was dead, or because the dead didn't matter, or because she was practicing for cheerleading, Morgan didn't know. Mr. Fielding wandered back in. Remy had wrapped herself so tightly in her jacket, she might have been bandaging cracked ribs.

He wanted Remy to be okay.

It would be wrong to tell. It would not bring back Denise Thompson. If he told, his life would be over. It wouldn't matter what he got on college boards. What college would take an application from a kid who had killed somebody?

It was just a sign. I didn't kill her. All I did was take a sign.

He went carefully back inside, refusing to turn around and look again at the moralizing exhibit on the grass.

"**H**ey, man," said Nickie behind him in the hall.

So he hadn't skipped school. "Nicholas," Morgan

95

acknowledged. He kept walking. Kept hoping, somehow, that he was not friends with Nickie again.

Nickie caught up to him. Morgan was on his way to Phys Ed. The halls were packed with boys leaving and arriving at locker rooms. Nickie muttered, "Weird, isn't it?"

The last word Morgan would have used was *weird*.

"I mean, *we did that*," said Nickie.

"Shut up."

"I think about it at night," said Nickie. "A person was alive and now she's not. We managed that."

"*Shut up*," breathed Morgan. It could not be pride he heard in Nickie's voice. Nickie could not be proud that he had "managed" to end a life.

"It's sort of the ultimate cool, isn't it?" said Nickie.

Morgan thought he might be having a seizure. The inside of his head changed colors and noises exploded between his ears. His balance shifted and he stumbled.

"Thing is," said Nickie, "my parents wouldn't understand." He took Morgan by the shoulders for emphasis. "We gotta shut up about it." Nickie gave him a light punch in the belly. "See ya," he said.

See you? thought Morgan. In my grave. I never want to see you again. I never want to think about you again. If it hadn't been for you we wouldn't have done that! It's your fault. You chose that sign.

He made it to the locker room and had to sit on the long, thin wooden bench that divided the lockers. His head wouldn't stay up. It felt as if his neck had gotten thinner, or been severed. He kept tipping.

The gym teacher was kneeling next to him. "Morgan?"

Morgan was afraid of speech. What if confession

96

popped out of him? What if, when the gym teacher only needed to know if Morgan was going to throw up, and if so, would Morgan please do it in the toilet, Morgan said, "I killed her"?

He rehearsed. Then, carefully, "I'm okay, I think." He had never been less okay.

"You sit out," said the gym teacher. The gym teacher also punched him lightly.

When Morgan finally managed to walk into the gym, and slid to the floor with his back against the wall, everybody else was doing a floor exercise. Basketballs sailed around like huge brown atoms in a science exhibit.

If he blamed Nickie, he didn't feel sick.

Lark bounced from subject to subject like fizz in a soda. She must not let anybody bring up the sign thing. They might think she had taken it. She did have a stop sign, courtesy of long-gone Joel.

The thing was, you couldn't tell one stop sign from another. She could not risk having anybody look among her belongings.

Lark did not want to get involved with some sort of murder thing. She was a junior. Time to think about colleges. She had a nice background. B average, high PSATs, lots of theater and dance.

Lark eyed Remy. Her best friend was stumbling around, visibly upset, complexion pasty, hands cold, speech slow. Remy was not destined to become an actress.

Lark would cool the friendship till things settled down.

* * *

"Sway to the left!" cried Mr. Willit. "Sway to the right!"

"This is not cheerleading," said Taft. "Try to be normal, Mr. Willit. We basses are compromising our masculinity by singing in chorus at all."

"This isn't cheerleading?" said Mr. Willit, his jaw dropping in shock. "Oh, no! Taft, why didn't you tell me sooner?"

Concert Choir was happy. Another skit was under way. The only question was who the victim would be.

"I'd like our normalcy representative up here, please," said Mr. Willit.

"He means you, Queen Joanne," said Chase.

Morgan had not been able to eat in two days. A humming noise occupied his skull. He said, "Come on, Mr. Willit. I'm normal. Doesn't that exempt me from being a cheerleader?"

Everybody laughed. He must have delivered the line okay.

Involuntarily his eyes flashed toward Remy. She was sitting very straight, back away from the chair, like a punishment. Behind her was a row of three tubas on stands, so she was displayed against curves of gleaming gold.

Mr. Willit jerked dramatically to a halt. "Is that a blush of interest I behold upon your face, Morgan?" he said.

The chorus loved it.

Run with it, Morgan ordered himself, be the joke, laugh along. Don't fight it, not now.

Mr. Willit patted Morgan's cheeks, testing for heat level in this blush. Everybody who could whistle did.

Remy said, "Where, when we need him, is the God who Restrains Music Teachers?"

Mr. Willit laughed with everybody else. "Remy," he said, "I kind of like you."

"Do we tell?" said Morgan.

That was their date. Remy wanted to be in his lap, in his arms, in his life, and instead she was in a mall, among shoppers and strangers and canned Christmas carols.

They stood in the vast multistoried center, decorated now for Christmas, although Thanksgiving had yet to arrive. A million glittering gold stars fell from invisible wires. High in a distant corner one star was much larger than the rest.

Mr. Willit kind of likes me, thought Remy Marland.

What would Concert Choir be like if he knew? If Mr. Willit kind of despised her. Kind of vomited at the thought of her.

Around them snaked a line of toddlers eager to sit on Santa's lap. "I know what I'd ask for," said Remy.

Morgan nodded. "I'd take the night back."

If only you could. It had been just a moment in their lives. It had no right, that moment, to have done so much without their consent.

Remy wanted the stars above to be stars of love. She wanted a kiss.

They slumped down on the pewlike curl of endless seating. Morgan put his arm around her. Her dreams for junior year had included just such an arm, in just such a place. She'd wanted to date Morgan, or a boy as terrific as Morgan, share movies and popcorn and have their favorite song, and she would wear his class ring on a ribbon around her neck. "Never mind, Morgan. You don't have to date me. I'm thinking of becoming a nun, anyway."

99

"We don't have nuns in our church," he said.

"I'm starting my own. It'll be for murderers and drug dealers and child abusers."

Morgan usually found tears the most horrible imaginable tool of womankind. This time, he was glad to see them. If she cried, he wouldn't.

After long uncivilized years in which Morgan would not use Kleenex, because his sleeve was quicker, he had adopted his father's habit of carrying a huge white cotton handkerchief. He handed it over. She pasted it over her face like a bank robber's mask.

"Remy, we didn't murder anybody. Okay, we were stupid and thoughtless. We were thieves and vandals. But we didn't know anybody would get killed. We didn't plan on Denise Thompson driving through that intersection."

Remy stayed behind her white curtain. "We should have."

"But we're not murderers. We're not drug dealers. We're not child abusers."

She dropped the curtain an inch. Her lovely teary eyes met his. "Then what are we, Morgan Campbell?"

He swallowed. "Nice kids who normally do the right thing?" Maybe she would smile and agree.

"Denise Thompson's still dead. You can never get by that."

Only their ski jackets were touching. And yet Morgan had never been so intimate with any person in his life. Perhaps he never would be again. No sex, no love, no act of fatherhood or war, would ever make him so close to another human being. He actually thought of marrying Remy, in order to seal up the guilt and keep it between them.

Get a grip, Campbell.

"If you want to tell," he said, "I'm ready."

They sat for a long time.

Shoppers swirled around them. Lights twinkled and carols played. Bright packages and stuffed shopping bags bounced against wool coats. Happy children and exhausted cranky children demanded to go to the Food Court.

"I'm actually thinking of marrying you," said Remy, "to keep the secret between us. We'd add an extra vow to our marriage ceremony."

He was staggered. He tried to say he'd just had that thought, but it was too scary to say out loud. She was braver than he was.

"I don't want to tell," said Remy. "I don't want anybody to think that's the kind of person I am."

She's not braver than I am, he thought. Neither one of us is brave at all.

He remembered himself long ago, last week, wanting danger, snipers, bombs, mountains, and thrills. *I'm not brave after all. I'm a coward.*

All that was on Monday.

Morgan had never endured such emotion and demand. Surely Tuesday would just lie there, letting him catch his breath, giving him time off to think about it.

Tuesday did.

Wednesday did not.

On Wednesday the local paper, to which Current Events subscribed in multiple copies, contained a full-page ad.

Full.

Paid for by Denise Thompson's husband.

Twenty-two inches by fourteen inches of heavy, screaming black type above a charming photograph of a pretty woman.

WHO MURDERED MY WIFE?
I DON'T KNOW BUT I WILL FIND OUT.
Look at this beautiful woman.
Only twenty-six.
You killed her.
You ended her life and left mine empty forever.
Don't sleep tonight. Lie there.
Think about my wife.
Think about my motherless son.
REWARD!
Tell me who murdered my wife.

CHAPTER 7

But it was the Wednesday before Thanksgiving. Everybody in America had Thursday and Friday off, the entire country having family reunions, turkey and stuffing.

Let Mr. Thompson put it in the paper only once, thought Remy. Don't let him run it again next week. Don't let anybody in Driver's Ed want a reward.

Mr. Thompson didn't give a dollar amount for the reward. What would it take for somebody to tell? A thousand dollars? Ten thousand dollars? Twenty-five dollars?

If Driver's Ed gets questioned, if they ask our parents who went out that night, if they search our houses . . .

. . . *don't let it happen.*

Who did she think was listening? She had run out of handy little gods.

Denise Thompson must have begged a fairy godmother or guardian angel to get her out of that intersection. And nobody had come to her aid. Why would one come to Remy's?

* * *

Morgan's father, of course, read every newspaper as well as watching every television newscast. He ripped out the ad before he recycled the paper and left it loosely folded on the coffee table. The bottom half hung where Morgan had to read it over and over.

> *Don't sleep tonight. Lie there.*
> *Think about my wife.*
> *Think about my motherless son.*
> REWARD!
> *Tell me who murdered my wife.*

It worked for Morgan. He didn't sleep.

Thanksgiving was the only holiday on which the scattered Marland family came together. Everybody drove Wednesday night to Aunt Marian's, bringing sleeping bags and air mattresses (except elderly relatives with hotel reservations). Remy, her brothers, her cousins, second cousins, and this year newly inherited cousins from a remarriage, all slept on the floor: a slumber party from infants (Henry) to college kids.

Aunt Marian provided the turkeys; it took three to feed the crowd. Remy's family was responsible for bread, and there were pumpkin rolls, corn spoonbread, cranberry muffins, buttermilk biscuits, and long, thin cylinders of French bread. They were oven hot, and set enticingly among them was room-soft sweet butter packed in pretty little bowls.

Grandmother Marland, who was deaf and confused, hugged each grandchild in a continual round of affection. It was like Driver's Ed; Remy got more than her fair share of hugs because Grandma could not remember how far down the line she had gotten, and stalled next to Remy. The family smiled and let it go. The unhugged kids reminded Grandma what their names were, and Grandma said, "Of course, darling, you've grown so much!"

They ate most of the day, taking seconds and thirds, with family gossip, television football, and outdoor games for the kids in between. Sleeping bags were finally unzipped around midnight, after the littlest kids had just collapsed on the floor, to sleep like cats wherever they gave up.

Remy tucked way down inside her sleeping bag. Cousins talked without her, mainly of cars. Who had a license; who was waiting for one; who had a car; who was saving for one; who had backed over a trike left in the driveway and who had gotten a speeding ticket.

The sleeping bag was safe and dark and warm. Inside, she let herself cry.

Denise Thompson had not just had a husband Mark and a son Bobby. Somewhere lived *her* mother and father. Brothers, maybe, and sisters. Cousins. Would Thanksgiving for Denise Thompson have been a family reunion? Had that family spent Thanksgiving weeping for the twenty-six-year-old who would never give thanks again?

Thanksgiving at home did not happen in the Campbell family. Morgan's mother believed hotels existed in order to save her from that kind of thing. Every year they went someplace special. This year it was Bermuda.

Morgan loved Bermuda. He loved the bicycling and the sand, the wind and the people.

It was a vacation of the mind.

Even Starr seemed desirable to Morgan those three days at the resort. She was good company, she laughed, she was nice.

He and Starr bicycled past a little intersection with no signs. No stop signs, no yield signs, no arrows or names.

Morgan pedaled on, trying to have no thoughts, to be nothing but legs pumping wheels.

All we did was take an octagon of wood off a post. It isn't my problem that somebody came along. A good driver would have known enough to stop even without the sign.

Starr was so far ahead of him that she turned, came back, and cycled in a circle around him, laughing. "Daydreamer," she said. "Are you in love? Tell me who it is."

How strange, thought Morgan, actually smiling at his sister, actually liking her. I'm the one, now, who is not nice.

Sunday they flew back.

Their four telephones combined had twenty-three messages blinking away and the fax had dumped page after page on the floor behind his father's desk.

One will be from the police, he thought. Somebody who wanted that reward told, and now somebody knows. In a few seconds Dad will know too.

The maid, who usually came Fridays, had not, since she, too, celebrated Thanksgiving. Mr. Thompson's ad still hung over the side of the coffee table. Starr was in her room on the phone, of course, having been unable to make calls for four whole days. He was momentarily alone. He picked up the ad without letting his eyes read the words, crushed it with both fists, and dropped it in the wastebasket.

His heart was at it again; it had a new hobby: it liked to double its speed. Just when he thought he was faking it fine, his heart would betray him. Thrum like bass guitar strings.

Morgan did not have long to wait. Dad slammed out of his office, door hitting doorstop with a rubbery thud. This is it, thought Morgan, he's going to throw me up against the wall, break my arm—

"The news is next," said Dad, jogging past. "Get those televisions on. I lost the whole world on Bermuda. This is it for vacations. I hate being isolated."

The room turned to water around Morgan. He had to swim to his seat, grabbing the sofa back as if it were the pool rim, trying to put bones back into his jellyfish body.

"Guatemala, Morgan!" shouted his father.

Morgan tried to recall a time when Guatemala had seemed important.

"Forty-three thousand refugees," said Anne of the silver hair, "have fled into Mexico, but some are beginning to return."

Morgan concentrated on refugees. It sure beat the other stuff he had to concentrate on. How did you even think about 43,000 people fleeing? Were they on the road, changes of clothing, loaves of bread, and two-year-olds under their arms? What did towns look like, with 43,000 people on their way out? Or in?

"Did you get that, son?" demanded his father.

"Yes, Dad. Thanks."

Compared to Guatemala, he said to himself, compared to 43,000 refugees wandering around, what's one car accident?

This calmed him for two minutes. He knew because he timed himself.

Maybe he could work up to more calm time, the way you worked up to more weights. He would add guilt-free minutes. Eventually he would get himself up to an hour, and then to twenty-four hours, and then he could forget about it.

It would be meaningless.

Just another traffic accident in the big road-slick of life.

Monday again.

Her second Monday since the stop sign.

Perhaps she would spend her life counting the Mondays since the stop sign.

The principal of East Line High took his duties seriously. He had put Mr. Thompson's ad on the main bulletin board.

WHO MURDERED MY WIFE?
I DON'T KNOW BUT I WILL FIND OUT.
Look at this beautiful woman.
Only twenty-six.
You killed her.
You ended her life and left mine empty forever.
Don't sleep tonight. Lie there.
Think about my wife.
Think about my motherless son.
REWARD!
Tell me who murdered my wife.

"Today," said Mr. Fielding, "I will drive with Taft, Chase, and Remy."

Remy held her name tag up to signify willingness to switch. She wanted to stay in the library and hear the gossip and the guesses.

Incredibly, Mr. Fielding saw the motion. "Yes, Remy," he said, reading off her tag. "You."

"Hasn't she done more driving than anybody else?" complained Joss, who had been planning to take her place.

Mr. Fielding was confused: how could one person do more driving than another? Taft, Chase, and Remy followed him out of the library and past Mrs. Bee.

Taft drove. Exiting the school campus meant coming close to the wreck. Remy wiped tears from her cheeks.

"You're taking this so hard," said Taft. "You didn't know Denise Thompson, did you?"

I killed her. Does that count?

Chase said, "I think about it all the time. And to think that our class actually—"

"Shut up," said Taft.

Lark's eyes regarded Morgan. They were just eyes, not attached to Lark at all, but as if she had popped them in that morning. They did not blink, they did not drift away, they were fastened on him.

Morgan braced himself. This was it. Lark was going to talk about it. She was going to say, So, Morgan, what signs did you and Nickie and Remy steal that night I knew better than to go along?

Alexandra leaned way forward and swung her yellow hair, so it grazed Morgan's shoulder. "So, Morgan," she said flirtily, "what are you getting me for Christmas?"

Morgan was truly astonished. "Me?"

He knew Christmas was coming. He had the pageant rehearsal schedule from Mrs. Willit. Sunday night he and his mother had taken the boxes of decorations down from the attic. Starr had stacked CDs to play the endless rounds of Christmas carols Mom would want playing for the next four weeks.

But presents? For Alexandra?

"So far," announced Alexandra, "I am considering getting you a calendar of girls who win weight-lifting championships, or else a calendar to increase your vocabulary."

"Why do I need a calendar?"

Alexandra kissed his cheek.

His mouth fell open as if he expected her to feed him.

"I'm giving you a calendar," said Alexandra, "so you'll have plenty of room to jot down the dates you and I are going out."

Morgan could not recall the slightest suggestion on his part that he might date Alexandra. "Mr. Willit was right. I'm going out with Remy," he said quickly. He hoped he would get to Remy before the rest, to let her know.

The class went nuts. "You *are*?"

"That's so neat!"

"Why didn't you say so?"

"She didn't tell me!"

This was entirely from girls. The boys were paralyzed. Morgan's involvement with girls might spread, and contaminate them.

"A Driver's Ed romance," said Joss, clasping her hands like an illustration on a Valentine's card. "Ooooh, Morgan, I love it! Did it start in the backseat? With Mr. Fielding as chaperone?"

How incredible, thought Morgan. We're not going to talk about the ad. We're not going to mention the sign.

He suddenly wondered if other members of the class had gone out that Thursday night and taken their own stop signs.

"Stay in the slow lane, Taft," said Mr. Fielding. It's one of my kids, he thought. He had half heard the giggly talk of sign stealing. He half knew who did the mailbox bashing too.

Half listening was key. Then he could hold himself only half responsible.

My kids.

He never thought of his classes that way anymore. They were other people's kids, in whom he had no interest and whose lives he assumed would never again intersect with his.

But there was a scrap of teacher left in him. A piece, he was surprised to find, large enough to cut. Oh, dear God, he thought, when did I stop being a teacher?

His kids had done these things. His kids, whose names he did not bother to learn, whose driving he did not bother to supervise, whose faces he made no effort to remember.

It was one of the Cristin/Kierstin/Christine crowd. One of the watery blondes who knew the rules for mailbox baseball.

I was a good person once, he thought. I was like Matt Willit. I was passionate. I taught and they learned. Why did I stop teaching math? Why did I turn to Driver's Ed where nothing matters?

But that's the problem, isn't it? he thought. It matters most, and I didn't care.

"Turn onto Cherry," he said to Taft, "and pull over."

He did not glance at Taft to see the boy's expression.

They got out of the car. The double post still stuck up out of the dirt: six feet of it, the top rudely sliced. Temporary blinking yellow lights on a sawhorse marked the intersection now.

Remy, Taft, Chase, and Mr. Fielding grouped around it, hands folded like people gathered at a grave. Mr. Fielding felt as if he had been at a stop sign of his own for a long time. Half dead, still teaching. Not as dead as Denise Thompson.

"Who took it?" said Mr. Fielding.

Do not panic, thought Remy. He's guessing. He can't even tell us from Chrystal, Carson, and Joanne. Stand still, stay calm.

"How would we know who took it?" said Taft. He moved restlessly, watching his feet as if trying to learn a dance step. Mac did that when he was guilty of something. Was Taft guilty of something or were his feet cold? Or was Taft protecting her?

They stood on the half-frozen ground until Mr. Fielding tired of staring at the post. Nobody said anything else.

Nance Campbell adored Christmas. Parties were warmer, greetings were gayer, laughter was kinder. She had a collection of decorations from all around the world. Stars and angels, candy canes and icicles and camels and candles. It took the entire first weekend in December, all four Campbells working, to decorate the house. Real holly was wound up the banisters, and wreaths hung from every door.

On their way home from the *Nutcracker* ballet it actually snowed a little. Flurries that didn't count, but made Morgan's mother happy. "Do you think we might actually have a white Christmas this year?" she said dreamily.

Dad was a ridiculous romantic. One snowless December, Dad had actually trucked in snow as a Christmas gift for Mom.

"Did you name me for Christmas, Mom?" said Starr. She asked this a lot because she liked the answer.

"I wanted a name," said their mother softly, "that rang and sang."

Morgan wondered what the ringing and singing would be like if they found out about the stop sign.

Dad tapped the automatic garage door opener on the visor and the long wall of the two-car garage lifted. The BMW pulled in next to the Range Rover. The garage doors closed silently behind them, and they went indoors.

What would little Bobby Thompson's Christmas be like? Had his dead mommy already bought presents? Would Santa bring Bobby presents from a dead woman?

And Mr. Thompson, taking out those ads.

What would his Christmas be like?

His mother surprised Morgan with an intense hug, stepping back to hold his face possessively. He let her do this, and she hugged him again. "I'm so happy," she said. "You know how sometimes your family seems perfect and the day was just right and Christmas is coming?"

She and Dad waltzed the rest of the way down the hall, through the living room and the dining room and into the front hall and through the kitchen and into the family room and back.

"Yuck," said Starr succinctly, vanishing upstairs before she got dragged into this.

How much older Starr seemed in that dark green velvet skirt.

Denise Thompson would never get older.

"Dad," he said, during the first slew of ads before the late news, "do you believe in church or are you just going because you're running for office?" He recognized a flicker of hope in his father's eyes, that this difficult son was addressing him. Not exactly your basic easy question, but still—speech.

"I guess," said his father, "the more responsibility you take on—or, in my case, *want* to take on—the more help you need. Our state . . . has every problem there is. Race riots, lousy schools, collapsing bridges, second-rate hospitals, more immigrants than we can house. I have plans . . . but . . ."

Give me a way out, Morgan thought. A sign that I don't have to worry about the sign.

"I don't know what I believe," said his father. "I don't think most people know for sure. I only know that words of wisdom that have helped for thousands of years help me too."

"Like what?"

His father quoted the Bible. Easily, as if he used the words all the time. "Like Micah. *And what doth the Lord require of thee, but to do justly and love mercy.*" The news came back on. "It helps me decide things, to say that in my mind," said his father.

Morgan could not recall his father ever before uttering a sentence when the anchor was talking.

If the Lord requires Dad to do justly, thought Morgan, and if justice is prison . . . On the other hand, if the Lord also requires mercy . . . how much justice and how much mercy would I get?

If it's up to Dad, I guess there would be some mercy. If it's up to the husband, it would be all justice and no mercy. But I don't blame him. I'd kill me, too, if I were the husband.

Mom slipped into the room, sitting next to Dad and leaning on him squishily.

The next ad was not for soft drinks or cars.

It was not an ad for profit or sales.

It was Mr. Thompson's ad.

Morgan's thickened fingers were so useless, he could not wrap them around his Pepsi can. It slid out of his grip, down the edge of the sofa and onto the floor. Nothing spilled. It stayed upright. It was doing better than Morgan.

The guy was paying for television time? Where did he get the money? What did he hope to accomplish?

The ad was narrated by a masculine voice that trembled with a rage Morgan well recognized. Adrenaline screaming for action, muscles requiring that he pound out of a room.

A home video, blurry and off center, filled the screen.

Denise Thompson knelt on the green grass of summer, her arms out, her hair blowing, while her little son Bobby staggered toward her. Red toddler pants, snaps on the inseam. Bobby's hair and eyes were the same color as his mother's.

His dead mother's.

What have I done? How can I undo it? There must be a way to undo it!

Morgan tried to remember even a single verse from

115

his years of Sunday school, even a single word that would help him the way Micah helped his father.

Morgan's living mother sipped her drink. "I agree with you, Rafe. Whoever took that sign should be shot."

CHAPTER 8

"A family conference?" said Morgan warily. He was the only family in the room.

Mr. Bailey had organized Dad's last campaign. Mr. Bailey laughed heartily, to show that he had been sixteen once. "We're on the same team, Mor, and we have to work up our plays."

Morgan sat carefully on the couch. He and Mr. Bailey were in the rarely occupied formal living room. On the mantel were photographs of Morgan and Starr at various stages of braces and slow development. Morgan often considered burning the family photos.

"The thing is, Mor," said Mr. Bailey, "you and I know that this family is beautiful. Really beautiful." Mr. Bailey shook his head a few times to show how mind-boggling the Campbell beauty was. "But every now and then a closet that looks clean and neat is stuffed with skeletons. And the people donating to this campaign, people that have money riding on this—they like to know. Every skeleton falls out, Mor. No matter how tight you close that door, the media get in through the cracks. So there can't be any secrets, you know what I mean?"

His hands were puffy again, the blood from his chest rushing to his fingers, to make him sign a confession. "I guess," he said. He hated being called Mor.

"Now, a sixteen-year-old hasn't had time to put many skeletons in the closet, Mor." Mr. Bailey laughed.

Morgan could see his skeleton perfectly: the long white bones of a twenty-six-year-old named Denise Thompson.

"So," said Mr. Bailey. "You ever try drugs? Who'd you buy them from?"

Morgan wondered if anybody had ever told Mr. Bailey anything. And if so, why?

"It's okay, son. We elected a president who tried marijuana. You can tell me about it. That's why your mom and dad aren't in the room. It's just you and me, so we can line those skeletons up and put 'em out of business. You know what I mean?"

Mr. Bailey went on about alcohol and drugs, like the films in Driver's Ed. "So you can assure me," said Mr. Bailey, his face so close that Morgan had to lean backward to escape, "there is no scandal we have to worry about with you."

"Scandal" sounded middle-aged. Men and women with pasts. "All I do is go to school."

Mr. Bailey nodded down at his notebook and seemed to check data on Morgan. "That's true," he said. "Don't have your driver's license yet, do you?"

Maybe he should throw the driver's test. The way boxers throw matches. Couldn't be that hard to fail. Then he wouldn't get his license, which he didn't deserve. "Another few weeks."

Mr. Bailey grinned widely. "Then we'll have to keep an eye on you, won't we?"

Morgan grinned back. He wondered if the grin looked like Lark's. Too tight for his mouth. "Yes, sir."

Mr. Bailey whapped him on the shoulder blades. "Great talking to you," he said. "I'm really really really excited about this campaign. We're gonna win, I can feel it, your dad can feel it. How about you, Morgan, can you feel it?"

If he told what he was feeling, everything would get sucked down and drowned in the whirlpool of his stupidity.

Morgan collected his shepherds and handed out staffs. The church had a nice staff collection after so many pageant years. Everybody liked to hook everybody else's ankles and yank them down at crucial spots.

This happened only in rehearsal. During the real thing, Christmas Eve, every year, it was real. The kids really were shepherds and the baby really was Jesus. On Christmas Eve, when the congregation sang "It came upon a midnight clear," the shepherds would shiver, full of belief.

This, however, was rehearsal. The boys could hardly wait for the third line in the song, "peace on the earth, goodwill toward men," so they could bellow the time-honored substitution, "piss on the earth."

The crèche was up. Bales of hay rested below the altar. Kings' costumes were draped over the first pew.

That's what I did, Morgan thought. Pissed on the earth.

"Mom!" bellowed Mac. "We could bake pottery in here! Turn down the heat!" She didn't, so he leaned between the front seats to adjust the car heater himself.

"Remy, when you get your license, I'm in charge of temperature," he said to his sister.

She didn't even hear him. Remy's crush on Morgan Campbell was sickening. How could his own sister fall for one of those blond preppies of perfection? Now she was even going down to the church on a Thursday afternoon to help polish the Christmas silver, a feeble excuse to feast her eyes on Morgan at a dumb old pageant rehearsal. Everybody but goody-goody Mrs. Willit saw through Morgan. "Pageant Director" would look good on his college application.

"Mom, you know that wrecked car on the high school lawn?" said Mac. He gave Matt an Oreo cookie because then Matt would be completely covered with chocolate saliva by the time they reached the church. "The one where the woman was killed because somebody stole the stop sign? I'd sue 'em, that's what I'd do. Sue 'em for a million bucks."

"If it was kids, they don't have any money," said Mom.

Mac shrugged. He knew about deep pockets. "The parents do. I say sue 'em." It dawned on Mac that Remy did not have free Thursday afternoons. "Hey, Remy, what about basketball practice?"

"I quit."

Mom practically went off the road. "What?" she cried. "Remy! You quit basketball? Are you serious?"

"Yes."

"You quit JV?"

"Yes."

"Why? Tell me why! Your father and I love those games, Remy! How can you do this to us?"

"I'm not good enough."

This was true, and yet because Mac knew either everything about his sister or nothing, and in this case it was everything, he knew that she was lying. She had not quit because she was lousy at it. So she had quit her basketball team, after all these years of effort and practice, in order to hang out and stare at Morgan!

"Sue her," Mac told his mother helpfully.

Remy could not figure out why nobody from Driver's Ed had called in to get the reward Mr. Thompson was offering. Money motivated people. Look at Mac, so eager to sue, to hop on that good old American bandwagon, grab his share in the lawsuit. Any lawsuit.

Last night she had stood in front of the mirror staring at her hair: the short quick gold hair she usually approved of. A single strand had grown too long. She cut it off with embroidery scissors and suddenly wanted to cut it all off, hack it off, scrape it off, look hideous and ridiculous and guilty. She had stood trembling, a hank of hair in her left hand, scissors held open in her right.

She had not done it. The thing was to blend in, to be one of the crowd, as invisible to the world as she and her classmates were to Mr. Fielding.

"I don't want Henry being Jesus this year, Mom. Let them use a doll. Or the Van Holland baby. You know Henry won't behave. You know he's more like a difficult pet than a person."

"Remy!"

"Well, he is! Stop pretending he's different from anybody else's one-year-old. He's all mess and noise and smell."

Mom parked at the church back door. The church was pure white, reassuringly symmetrical whether you came in at the back, side, or front.

Somebody would call Mr. Thompson. Somebody would want money enough to do it. Remy didn't want it on TV that the Marland family was so screwed up, one kid was out there killing while the other was playing Jesus.

Starr had been an angel for years. At last she'd get the scarlet cape, which would fill the aisle behind her like a princess's wedding train. "Ugh, you two are the other kings?" said Starr, gagging at the sight of Roger and Kyle.

"I'm only kinging because my mother's making me," said Kyle.

"And I get the red one, Starr, so keep your mitts off it," said Roger.

"Morgan!" screamed Starr. "I get the red cape."

The sheep got down on their hands and knees and the shepherds herded them with resounding whacks on exposed limbs.

Mrs. Marland set the baby down. Henry took off at full speed, which was a lot faster than Morgan expected. Henry crashed into a pew, picked himself up, climbed onto the pew, clambered along it, fell off, opened a hymnbook, tore out pages, crawled out of reach, laughed joyfully, crawled under the next pew, and found another hymnbook to deface.

This is Jesus, thought Morgan. Wonderful. Maybe we could sedate him prior to the pageant. Jesus the tranquilized.

"Remy," said Mrs. Willit affectionately, "I can always count on you. Who else would agree to do this?"

Remy had propped the kitchen door, the hall door, and the sanctuary door open so she could watch Mor-

122

gan as she polished. When Morgan saw her, they waved Royal Family waves back and forth.

Her heart turned over.

Going out with Morgan. I wonder if we actually will. Go out, that is. Or if we'll just say so to other people, and lie, and lie, and lie some more.

Our wave, thought Morgan. Our joke. Our stop sign.

The stop sign had moved. It was not hidden in the basement. It was between him and Remy. He wanted to steal it a second time—destroy it—set fire to it. Anything to go on with life.

And every time he thought that, he remembered that Denise Thompson could not go on with her life.

Generations ago somebody had given the church Christmas silver: plates and chalices heavily embossed with stars. It had been lying around for decades getting black with tarnish. Mrs. Willit wanted to use the stuff this year. She and Remy struggled with polish, old toothbrushes, paper towels, soap and water.

"I love how tarnish disappears," said Mrs. Willit, admiring the sparkle. "Isn't it a great metaphor? From tarnish to treasure. I'll use that in my next sermon. Polish takes away sin."

Remy, whose hand was full of filthy paper towels, stared at Mrs. Willit and knew something.

Mrs. Willit had never done anything wrong. Oh, she'd probably been mean to somebody once, or even shoplifted a lipstick. But if she had done anything truly wrong, she'd know polish didn't take anything away. It just moved it around. And saying you're sorry—that didn't take anything away. Didn't even move it around.

Remy was sorry, and Denise Thompson was still dead.

Remy hadn't even read the single word on that sign, had done nothing by intent, and Denise Thompson was still dead.

"Come on, Remy, let's go," said her mother. "I'm still provoked with you for quitting basketball. It ruined the whole rehearsal for me."

Henry had reached the toddler stage of exhaustion in which nothing was left but whining. Only sleep could solve his problems but he was too hungry and too wired. They'd have to endure his screams and sobs and hitting until he collapsed.

Remy rubbed his little back, which sometimes calmed him.

I could baby-sit for Bobby Thompson, she thought. I have lots of experience. I could work off guilt that way. Kind of like going to a gym and working off flab.

How obscene. She would snuggle a little boy whose mother lay in a grave because of her?

She held Henry before putting him in the car seat, and pressed her face against his, so their tears blended. *Oh, God!* she thought, and it was no prayer to a little local deity, it was to the real one. The big one. But there was no answer.

Car pools consumed the children in batches. Shepherds returned their crooks by hurling them across the church like javelins. The bales had been torn open, and hay was strewn around as if camels had been put up for the night.

Christmas! Morgan thought, swearing. He wondered who had given Starr a ride home and why they

hadn't waited for him. Life had broken down into in-
stallments, payment after payment.

Tonight was the first of several Campbell Christmas
parties. Tonight was lawyers. Lawyers under the tree,
lawyers by the punch bowl, lawyers singing carols, lawyers opposed to carols.

Morgan thought of presidential hopefuls and the
secrets they had thought hidden, or had forgotten
about, or hadn't known were important. TV found out,
and the candidates were ruined. From New York to Los
Angeles, from Chicago to New Orleans, America said,
"Ugh, kick him out."

I have to know, thought Morgan, if my parents
would kick me out.

He had a dim sense of no longer knowing what the
Campbell family was, or why it existed. No longer
knowing what love was, or whether it existed.

In the church kitchen, between the stretch of ovens
and dishwashers, was a telephone. LOCAL CALLS ONLY, it
said, which ensured that everybody in Sunday school
would make long-distance calls.

Morgan's was local.

He called Nicholas. "I have to tell."

Nicholas stood very still.

His family was not religious, and for them Christmas was stockings, poinsettias, and lots of shopping.

His mother was Frisbee-ing junk mail across the
kitchen into the open trash can and his father was cir-
cling Christmas-tree ads in the paper. They always cut
their own tree. Dad liked to pick a tree farm at a pretty
big distance, so getting it would be an event.

Nicholas scoffed at this. You could drive to the cor-

125

ner, point to a tree, and have them deliver. Even when he was eight or ten, Nickie was too old for such nonsense. Now he was seventeen and he thought, I'm too young. I can't have this happening to me. Morgan is going to tell? Does he have any idea what will happen to us?

He held the phone loosely, trying to be casual. What could he say with his mother and father in the room while he talked?

Tell, and I'll kill you, Morgan. No, wait, I'm coming over. I'm going to kill you first, before you tell. Anyway, I won't admit I was there. Me? Drive that jerk Morgan around? Give me a break. I'll lie, Morgan. It'll be all you. And what about Remy, huh? You going to haul Remy into this? Going to ruin her life?

But the room was full of parents. There was nothing Nicholas could say, not a word.

His mother handed him a Christmas card to read while he talked on the phone: old neighbors who had moved to Kansas and said the schools were better.

Nicholas said to Morgan, "Not yet. Let's talk about it first."

I'll kill him. I have to get rid of him. He can't tell. It would kill my parents.

Remy extricated Henry from the car seat. Of course, when Henry was in such a bad mood, he would not be carried, but also refused to walk. When she finally got Henry in and set him on the floor, she had to barricade him with her knees till she got the door locked behind them.

She loved that moment of safety when the door closed tight against the dark and the chill. She had not even had time to feel warm, to know that houses were good, and furnaces were best, when Mac yelled, "Call Nicholas. He says it's important. He says Morgan is going to tell."

Henry screamed to be picked up, lifting his arms and jumping against her. He tried to hook his little fingers in a tear in her jeans to yank her down to his level.

"What'll Nickie tell?" said Mac.

"Gossip."

"Tell me first."

"No." Remy ran to her room. Shivering and trembling, she stared at the extension.

Oh, God! she thought again, and then he was in the room with her—God was—suffocating and horrifying —somebody she did not want around at all—some grim, vengeful God from some ancient time, who would use a scythe and cut off her hands.

Remy picked up the phone, but called Morgan, not Nicholas.

Mrs. Campbell answered. "Hello, Remy, dear. Morgan just got in. Won't it be wonderful when you two have your licenses? And you don't have to arrange chauffeurs or miss rides? I understand your test is next week."

Small talk. Please. "Yes, it is."

"Are you excited?" said Mrs. Campbell, excited.

"Oh, yes."

"I'll be thinking about you, Remy. I know you'll pass."

"Thank you."

Phones were exchanged.

"Hello, Remy," said Morgan.

127

She leaped into it feet first. "Morgan, don't. Don't tell. You can't. Please. There's nothing we can make better by telling."

"It's just that I'm having a hard time thinking about anything else."

"Me too—but, Morgan, I keep looking at my family. You're letting Henry be Jesus again and my mother is so happy and here her darling daughter goes out and kills people."

There was a weird sound, not out of the phone, but behind Remy. A sort of sucking, like a small vacuum cleaner. She whipped around, and there stood Mac, who had breathed in so fast, he had choked himself.

She looked into her brother's eyes and saw that she had just achieved a childhood dream: she had shocked Mac.

"You took the stop sign?" said Mac. "*You?*"

CHAPTER 9

Now someone knew.

And not just any someone. A someone who loved to make trouble on purpose. Her own worthless, rotten brother.

"It's my fault, Remy," said Morgan. His voice was so tired, it didn't seem to take up the whole line. "You didn't actually take the stop sign. You didn't actually take any of them. I won't bring you into it."

She was weirdly angry with him. "Don't you free me from blame, Morgan Campbell. Don't you carry this all by yourself!" Her tears rushed down as if they had places to go, people to see. "Mac, don't you tell!"

Her brother was stunned. "You and Nicholas and Morgan took it?" said Mac.

"Listen," said Morgan. "I'll leave you out of it. I promise. It's just that . . . ah, Remy . . . I have to tell."

"You don't have to, Morgan!" She was twisting back and forth, keeping her eyes on Mac, so he wouldn't run and find Mom, and concentrating on Morgan, so she'd win the argument. "They can't find out, Morgan. Let it lie there."

Let it lie there. Remy was piling sin upon sin, like blankets on beds. She would be the princess in the fairy tale, the little green pea of her terrible deed always at the bottom of her sleep. She would never again get through a night.

Morgan was still silent, and she knew that he would tell. He had to tell. It was going to come out of him like vomit purging itself from a sick stomach. "At least wait until you and I can talk it over, Morgan. Not on the phone. Holding hands."

Maybe holding hands with her was the last thing on earth he wanted, but if she could hang on to him, maybe they would make it.

After a long silence he said that he couldn't tell his parents tonight anyway because of an important Christmas party. So, okay, he would wait until tomorrow. Tomorrow they would meet and talk about it. "My father will drive us to the mall. I'll tell him I'm taking you to the movies. Eight screens, there's got to be a movie we'd want to see. First we'll talk."

An important Christmas party, thought Remy, hanging up slowly to postpone dealing with Mac.

Lovely sweet crystal-clear Christmas. Why couldn't this have happened before some stupid holiday, like Arbor Day or something? Why did it have to touch Christmas?

She stared at her brother. He was so short and thin. So achingly little for an eighth grader. If knowledge gave him power, she couldn't see it. "Just tell me if you're going to tell," she said fiercely.

He shook his head.

Remy sank onto her bed, and her brother sank down beside her. Clumsily, Mac patted her back. More clumsily, he put his arm around her and tried to hug. They were definitely amateurs at showing affection.

But, oh, how it counted! She actually rested her head on his lower, smaller shoulder. "Mac, it was such fun! Morgan and I were having so much fun."

"You never thought of what might happen?" he whispered.

"I thought of what might happen to *me*. I never thought of what might happen to *her*." She was clinging to him now. "Oh, Mac! Why couldn't Denise Thompson remember the crossing? Why couldn't she have driven home a different way? Why did there have to be such a big truck coming? If she'd hit some lightweight little Chicken McNugget of a car, she'd be alive."

I'm starting to hate the woman I killed, thought Remy. Like it's her fault. Little by little I'm not nice anymore. I want to be a nice person!

Her brother's voice was not junior high. Not taunting or teasing or obnoxious. It was sad. "You're in trouble now, Rem," he said, as if he loved her, and was willing to be in trouble with her.

"Not if we don't tell. Oh, Mac, they really could sue us. Or put us in jail. But not if we don't tell. The odds are they can't find out unless we admit it! So we're not telling."

Mac was quiet for a long time. "I think you're in trouble whether you tell or not," he said at last.

"You gotta understand something," said Nickie.

Nickie was smoking. Any minute the party guests would begin to arrive and it was entirely possible that Morgan's parents would glance out the window and see Nickie in their driveway. Mom and Dad hated both Nickie and cigarettes. Nickie was sucking slowly and

131

grandly, rotating smoke in his mouth, shifting his jaws, as if his smoke had more substance than other people's smoke and required space.

Nickie leaned on the Buick's open door, midswagger. He used the cigarette as a pointer.

"I'm not gonna get hooked into this," said Nickie. "You can't prove a thing, Morgan. You're the one has that sign, remember. And in case you didn't know it, every sign has a code number on the back, so the traffic department can identify it. It isn't just any stop sign you got in your cellar, buddy. It's *the* stop sign."

Nickie grinned. His teeth were separated, fanglike. His clothes fit even worse, as if he had grown over the weekend. How could he not notice that everything was too small on him? Didn't it make him crazy to have his pants halfway up his calf?

"You chose the sign," said Morgan. "You picked that stop sign. You and I both took it."

"You're lying, Morgan. And if you say I had anything to do with this, I'll ruin you." He was calm. He was making no threat. Ruining Morgan was a fact.

Nickie sounded primitive, and yet modern. Like one of the terrible civil wars they kept studying: where brothers and cousins decided Yes, this is the day we'll shell the neighbors, murder the firemen, kill the schoolchildren, and bomb the hospital.

Morgan got sarcastic. "I should wear a bulletproof vest? Have somebody taste my food?"

Nickie smiled and in that instant Morgan saw why parents didn't want their kids near Nickie Budie. "I'll make it worse," said Nickie gently. He spread the words through a swirl of gray smoke. The smile grew on his face and the smoke hung like the smile. "I'll tell the police, and your parents, and your friends, and all those

132

teachers you cozy up to, that you were *hoping* there'd be an accident. That's the kind of person you are, Morgan. You hung around the intersection, Morgan, and when it happened, you watched. You enjoyed yourself when Denise Thompson bought it."

Politics drew lawyers. Campaigns and publicity excited them. The Campbell house, magnificently decorated for Christmas, was packed with lawyers. Morgan was always slightly surprised to be reminded that his father as well as his mother was a lawyer.

Men and women gathered round with puppy-dog excitement. If they'd had them, tails would have wagged continually. Instead they ran their mouths. They were lawyers, they had to talk. They couldn't say anything once, they had to say it twelve ways.

CNN, mute, ran on one television, while the stereo played Christmas carols sung by English boy choirs. A lawyer with a weight problem turned the TV channel. "I want to see if the guy runs the ad again," he said.

Morgan was passing hors d'oeuvres. His tray had bacon-wrapped mushrooms, shrimp-filled rolls, and miniature asparagus quiches. He kept the tray steady.

The lawyer put three little quiches on a red-and-green napkin and speared a mushroom with a toothpick.

Let it be a car ad, thought Morgan, who knew perfectly well it was not a car ad. All these guests were already driving the car of their dreams.

Few were deflected from their wine and conversation. Only Morgan and the heavyweight lawyer glanced at the screen.

The ad came on.

Once more Morgan watched Denise Thompson

133

hold out her arms, and once more listened to the end of the story: Bobby Thompson would never hug his mother again.

Morgan's parents were over by the tree, telling where they had acquired their crystal star collection. This one in Paris, this one in San Francisco, this one in a darling little gift shop on the Cape.

"What would happen to the people who took that stop sign?" said Morgan very casually. "If they were ever found, I mean?"

Morgan's lawyer jumped right in and chewed on it. The man actually flexed his forehead wrinkles. "It's an interesting legal question. Taking a sign is only a misdemeanor. A larceny."

Morgan set the tray down, locked his fingers together, and studied his white knuckles. "You mean it's no big deal?"

"Maybe a fine. Fifty bucks. Unless you get into reckless endangerment."

Morgan felt his way. "And if there is reckless endangerment? Would they go to jail?"

The lawyer swallowed a baby quiche whole, like a raw oyster, chasing it with wine. He shrugged. "It's probably kids. Probably no priors. It'd be very rare for a juvenile with no priors to do time. They might get a felony sentence. One to five."

One to five. As in *years*. One to five *years*! Out of his life!

But that was fair. Denise Thompson, after all, had no years.

"With kids, though," said the lawyer, stabbing a toothpick through a mushroom as if he were executing it, "none of it would be served."

"None?"

The lawyer shook his head. "Never happen. Kid would get probation and community service."

They had been joined by a law partner of his mother's. She also took a baby quiche, but nibbled hers crumb by crumb. They were about to get a second opinion. That was fine with Morgan. He wanted to hear again about how none of the five years would be served.

"Your dad would like to see that changed, Morgan," she said. "The system is stacked so that criminal teenagers rarely end up paying for what they do wrong. Not in money. Not in prison terms. Not in public shame. Say the person who took that sign is a male minor, which is probably the case. You prove it, but you can't even get the boy's name in the newspaper or on television to shame him, never mind jail time. What's the penalty? Basically, see, in this case, a woman dies and the kid responsible for her death sails along on a fair wind."

"Now, wait. The law says he's not responsible," said the other lawyer. "He's responsible only for taking the sign."

"Correct," said the woman, "but the law and morality don't always cross paths. Anyway, your dad's idea, Morgan, is to put the parents' name in the paper instead. Make parents responsible. So they catch little Neddy Smith, who stole this sign, but little Neddy's name cannot be printed. So instead you get *this* into the paper: The fourteen-year-old-son of Joe and Mary Smith, who live at 150 South Main Street, was convicted today of the theft of, et cetera, et cetera. Joe teaches school at Center Elementary and Mary is a real estate broker." She finished her final crumb. "The parents, with any luck, lose some customers, some friends, and some standing in the community. At least somebody pays a price."

Over by the beautiful Christmas tree, glittering like one of her ornaments, Nance Campbell burst into peals of laughter. Her laugh was wonderful and room filling. Everybody turned to admire her.

The sixteen-year-old son of Rafe and Nance Campbell, of 1127 Farmington Avenue, was found guilty of stealing a stop sign, which resulted in the death of Denise Thompson. Nance Campbell is a prominent attorney. Rafe Campbell is running for governor.

Food Court at the mall. A thousand strangers having pizza wedges, egg rolls, curly french fries, or frozen yogurt. A thousand strollers with a thousand cranky babies, a thousand packages resting against a thousand knees. Morgan did not see how any of those people could have a problem as big as his.

"So in other words," said Remy, "we wouldn't go to jail, we wouldn't go to prison, we wouldn't get our names in the paper, and we wouldn't even pay much of a fine."

Morgan made piles of salt and pepper on the table and mixed them with a thin red-and-white-striped coffee stirrer. "Right."

"All that would happen is, our parents will hate us. Their lives will be ruined. Your father's campaign will end before it starts."

"That," said Morgan, "and Mr. Thompson will buy a shotgun and stalk us."

"Oh, well, then," said Remy. "What are we waiting for?"

They giggled hysterically. They were in a booth. They had started with Morgan on his side and Remy on hers, facing each other, but Morgan got brave and switched and was next to her now. Very next to her. The arm not lying on the table mixing salt and pepper was around her waist, pulling her in tight and warm.

Her left hand and his right balanced the glass shakers on their sides, tilted tepee-style over the salt.

Remy brushed her lips over his cheek.

He held her a little tighter. "But that's only the legal side," said Morgan. He let out his breath so hard, the salt blew in a tiny white hurricane across the slick table-top. "Now I have to tell you about Nickie."

Remy forced Henry into his high chair, but Henry was sick of the high chair and buckled his knees, curled his toes, and fought.

Using hands, elbows, and even chin, she tried to shove Henry down and jerk the tray in to hold him. Henry preferred sliding out the bottom. He slurped down like an otter until only his little nose showed above the tray.

"Some Jesus he'll make," Mac observed. "He's lying there as limp as a war protester. The only difference is, protesters don't drool."

Now the baby was panicking. He was too far down, couldn't get back up, and couldn't go out the bottom. "Come on, Matthew, baby, you can yell louder than that," Mac told him.

Remy got the tray loose, hung on to the baby's right arm, hauled him back, and set him upright. It was a miracle his arm wasn't stretched several inches by all this hauling around. Henry grinned his soppy four-toothed grin and started fighting the tray again. Remy whipped Henry on the third try and Mac smacked a bowl of Cheerios in front of him to keep him occupied.

"Mac!" yelled their mother. "He eats them dry!"

Mac had added milk. Henry joyfully splatted his fist down into the bowl. Milk and O's hit the wall. It was wonderful!

Dad, whose entrance was unheard over the shrieking and giggling and Cheerios-splatting, said, "I'm not sure that kid is really an A-one choice for Jesus this year."

"Morgan deserves better," agreed Remy instantly. She wanted Morgan's pageant to be perfect.

Henry stared in awe at the mess he had achieved and did it again, and managed it a third time before his mother could get in there and take the bowl away. What fun!

Too much laughing made Henry throw up, and sure enough, they leapt back with experienced timing and then had a good stirring fight about whose duty it was to clean the floor. Mac failed to see his responsibility in the matter.

"Remy, you have stars in your eyes," said Mom, laughing.

"Every time she sees vomit, she thinks of Morgan," explained Mac.

"You're dead, Mac Marland," said Remy. "You—" She heard herself. Mac heard her, too, and winced. *You're dead.*

"It's that serious?" said Dad, grinning. "Even Cheerios-throw-up is romantic to you now?" He hugged her. "I like a girl in love. I'm even going to forgive you for quitting basketball, although it's not going to be easy for me, and I want you to know how hard I'm struggling to continue loving you."

Oh, Dad! The struggle isn't here yet.

What if Nicholas carried out his threat? What if he told these parents of hers that Morgan and Remy waited to see if somebody would get killed? Enjoyed the entertainment event of the year?

No. Remy could not, *not*, let her parents hear Nickie's horrible suggestion. Because another horror had come to Remy.

They might believe him.

Starr answered the phone. She was so surprised by whatever she heard that she stared down into the receiver for a moment before she said anything. "It's Remy's mother, Morgan. For you."

Remy told, thought Morgan. Or Mac did.

He wasn't ready. A few hours ago he'd been ready; now he was totally unprepared. It was going to be like war, and Morgan needed to have his artillery. He felt exposed and weak.

"Oh, my goodness," said his mother. "You don't suppose something's happened, do you? Remy's hurt?"

"I love that!" said Starr. "They call Morgan when Remy goes into the hospital? That's so romantic." She rested her chin in her hands, looking at Morgan as if he were the cover of a romance novel, instead of a useless older brother.

"Is it true that Remy's real name is Rembrandt?" said his mother. "Or is that just one of those peculiar rumors that get started out of nothing?"

"Not only that," said Starr, "but her brother is named for the computer."

"Mac?"

"See?"

Mom burst out laughing. "You lie, Starr Campbell. Nobody, even people who call one kid Rembrandt and nickname another one Jesus, would name a kid Macintosh Computer."

Morgan was able to hold the telephone. He was even able to talk like a normal person. "Hello, Mrs. Marland."

"Ask her," whispered his mother, poking his ribs. "Find out why they named Mac Mac."

Morgan's hands were thickening again.

"We've decided Henry shouldn't be Jesus this year after all. Is it too late for you to use the Van Holland baby?"

His tongue lay like a dry napkin in his mouth.

"Sorry, Morgan," said Mrs. Marland. "We've taken a family vote and this kid is not manger-scene material this year."

"It's okay, Mrs. Marland," said Morgan. He was lisping, his mouth was so dry. "Maybe Henry is a little wild for Jesus."

"Jethuth," mocked Starr.

"Tell Starr she'll be a beautiful king," said Mrs. Marland, before she hung up.

"Starr, you'll be a beautiful king," said Morgan obediently.

His mother and Starr became distracted on a feminist theme: Should queens also have visited the baby in Bethlehem? Should the Bible possibly be revised to include queen visitation?

Morgan felt he had enough things to consider without that one. He retreated to the basement and his weights but even that was contaminated. The stop sign

140

was there with him. It was all but in his bloodstream now; in his sweat.

After the weights and before the rowing he walked over and looked at the back of the sign.

Nickie was right. It was numbered.

"Excuse me," said Mr. Willit.

The chorus knew from his voice that something was up. They smiled happily and shifted in their chairs with anticipation.

"May I have our Normalcy Representative up here, please?"

Morgan had no choice. He had to stand. Expose himself as Normalcy Representative. Everybody went into wave posture, and now he had to wave back, graciously and royally.

A terrible thing happened to him. He was perilously close to tears.

He waited for whatever joke or game the music teacher had in mind and thought of Nickie's threats.

The two people whose opinions he cared most about on earth were his father and Mr. Willit. If they heard those words . . . *He was hoping there'd be an accident, that's the kind of person Morgan is, he enjoyed himself when Denise Thompson bought it* . . . what would they think of him then?

And yet—what did anybody's opinion of Morgan matter? Whether they loved him or despised him, a woman was still dead.

"Beautiful, beautiful wave," said Mr. Willit. "Everybody on their feet, everybody wave, turn to page six, and take it from the top."

He saw me cave in, thought Morgan. He knows something is wrong, he let me off. What if he asks me to come in and talk? He's the kind of teacher who does that. Thinks he can get to the bottom of things and help.

Time had lost its usual spacing. Every minute lasted a century. Every night toppled down like falling dominoes, hitting him again with television news, adding night to night in which he had not yet told the truth.

The ads ceased.

Morgan's mother said poor Mr. Thompson probably ran out of money. "Or steam," said his father. "You can sustain that kind of rage only so long."

"And then what?" asked Starr.

"Then morning comes," said Dad. "You have a baby boy to bring up. Baby-sitters to find, macaroni and cheese to bake, *Goodnight Moon* to read out loud."

"I wanted to ask you, Starr," said their mother, switching the subject with the abruptness of a sneaky trial lawyer. "If Dad wins, would you want to stay and go to school here?"

"Here, of course," said Starr. "And why aren't you asking Morgan too?"

"It would be his senior year. We'd never disrupt that."

Disrupt it, thought Morgan. I'll go right now if you want. I'll be the advance team. I don't mind a few hundred miles between me and the intersection and Nickie.

"Forget it," said Starr. "I'm not starting at any new school."

"Where's your spirit of adventure?" said Mom.

"Let's win the campaign first," said Starr darkly.

"What are you going to do, Starr?" teased Dad. "Sabotage me?"

Everybody laughed, as if that were the funniest idea!

One of Dad's two kids! Sabotaging his campaign! Laugh, laugh.

Morgan saw the skeleton in their closet walk straight to the television stations. He saw the microphone at Nickie Budie's lips. His father ruined. Every dream and hope of both parents smacked down and run over by their own son.

CHAPTER 10

Remy Marland was the first to find out whether she was actually driver educated.

The night before, she spent in her closet, deciding what to wear for a driver's test. Twice she walked up to her mother, to say, "I can't be allowed to have a license," but she wanted the license, and she let her mother comfort her—"Now, darling, you'll do fine, they don't make you parallel-park anymore. Only twenty-four more hours, darling! It's a rite of passage, and you'll pass with flying colors, I know you will."

Remy thought of Denise Thompson's rite of passage.

She didn't meet Mac's eyes all night, because he knew too much. Remy had always thought it would be wonderful to be known, right down to the bone, to be understood and loved anyway. Well, it wasn't.

The class was wildly excited for her.

"Remember, the full stop has to be full," said Chase. "The car has to give that little jolt."

"Don't turn on the radio while you're actually driving," ordered Joss; "If you have to touch any control, wait till a red light. They don't like it if you do two things at once."

"They'll make you park at Super Stop and Shop," said Alexandra, "where the slots are extra thin, so leave yourself room to make it on the first try."

"And at the corner of Warren and Kennedy," said Kierstin, "there's *not* a right turn on red, even though it looks as if there ought to be, so don't make one."

Mr. Fielding, of course, gave Remy no advice.

"Don't forget to take off the parking brake!" said Taft.

"Remember I'm your first passenger," Morgan told her. "This afternoon. My house. You arrive complete with car and license. I'll be in the road thumbing a ride." He stood between the desks, combining a hitch-hiker's thumb with the royal wave. He was so handsome. So perfect. How could it be that the thing they shared was so imperfect?

"Give her a kiss," ordered Taft.

"Two kisses," said Lark.

He kissed her. It was such a careful, gentle kiss. His hand, curled in a light fist, strayed over her cheek and chin. "Do well," he murmured.

"Of course she'll do well," said Joss; "she's driven eight hundred times more than the rest of us."

"Which reminds me," said Lark, when Remy had left, "all money has to be in this afternoon because Christine's test is day after tomorrow."

"Have you ever driven at all, Christine?" asked Taft.

"Dad took me out twice. Mom took me out once."

"Christine, you can't take the test! Cancel it. Tell the truth."

145

"Since when," said Christine, "did anybody in this class ever tell the truth?"

The Motor Vehicle Bureau was on the opposite side of the city, between a large fitness center and discount appliance supermarket. It was just a storefront, as if you might buy shoes there. It hardly seemed possible that in such a building your life would change. In such a building, you would acquire your freedom.

Or not.

Remy curled and uncurled her fingers. In the end she'd worn the same faded blue jeans and baggy sweatshirt she'd had on almost all school days since September. She felt safe in them, protected by the fleece of the sweatshirt.

"You'll be fine," said Mr. Fielding. "You've been an excellent student."

How could he know who was excellent and who was not? He had never looked up. "Thank you," she said.

"I shouldn't teach this again," said Mr. Fielding. He rubbed his eyes, and rubbed them again. His voice was heavy and loaded. He was not talking to her like a teacher, but then, he never had, so Remy did not answer him like a student.

"No, Mr. Fielding. Probably not."

He held the door for her. "Kierstin has the stop sign, doesn't she? Lark had the idea, didn't she? Kierstin wanted a souvenir of Driver's Ed. The way Chase has his BIKE PATH collection."

Lines to renew licenses. Lines to get boat permits. Lines to acquire new plates. Lines to ask which lines to get in.

But Remy was scheduled and there was no line. No time in which to stand and think.

How many in Driver's Ed were slim blond girls in faded jeans and baggy sweatshirts?

Kierstin, Cristin, Lark, Remy, Alexandra, Christine.

The switching of name tags had for Mr. Fielding actually switched the personalities.

It made Remy feel interchangeable. As if the girls were appliances in boxes, marked the same, packaged the same. As if whoever bought them would get exactly the same item.

"Miss Marland?" The man was thick bodied, his glasses like Coke-bottle bottoms; he looked like the gork that Mr. Fielding was. "I'm Mr. Barth. I'll take you for your test."

They shook hands.

Mr. Fielding dropped into a chair.

She stood before the computer terminal. Thirty questions. She tapped her answers quickly and got twenty-six right. A solid pass. It was difficult to feel thrilled. It was difficult to feel anything. She could not even feel the sweatshirt fleece now. Mr. Barth led the way to Remy's car. He got in the passenger seat. Remy got in the driver's. Fastened her belt. Started the engine without grinding it. Took off the parking brake. Checked the rearview mirror. Backed out. Circled the lot.

She could not even feel her fingertips against the wheel. She, like the wheel, was made of plastic.

"Let's turn left onto Macey," said Mr. Barth, "and go straight for half a mile."

Macey had red lights every block, parallel parking, and hundreds of shops and businesses with entrances and exits. Remy slowed for people opening doors into her half of the road, for cars turning without signals, for yellow lights in the distance.

"And now let's turn down Wellstone," said Mr. Barth.

This led past an elementary school, but at this hour she would not have to worry about buses emptying or little kids dashing out under her wheels.

"And now on the interstate," said Mr. Barth.

She got on the interstate.

Would Mr. Fielding go to the police with his guess? Or to Mr. Thompson and the reward? Or would he let it drift? Maybe he had gotten it off his chest by speaking to Remy.

Why me? Do I give off an aura of maturity? Or was it just timing? Mr. Fielding reaching his limit on keeping secrets?

"And exit here," said Mr. Barth.

How she'd love to exit! Get off this problem. But there was no exit.

"And let's park between that Cadillac and that blue van."

Remy slid into the space.

But since Kierstin didn't do it, they can't prove anything. Besides, somebody like Kierstin would just elbow her way out. She'd be okay.

Except who could be okay after an accusation like that? From a sturdy source like your own Driver's Ed teacher?

People would say Kierstin just got away with it. Had a good lawyer.

And Kierstin's parents; her family. Would they get over it? Remy did not know Kierstin's parents. Some parents were very visible. You tripped on them continually from kindergarten through twelfth. Other parents might as well not have existed.

148

"Good work, Miss Marland," said Mr. Barth, opening his door. "You have passed your driver's test."

They were back at the Motor Vehicle Bureau. She had no recollection of coming back. No memory of traffic or road. Mr. Barth and the test might as well not have existed.

"Congratulations," said Mr. Barth.

"Tilt your chin up," said a bored wrinkled woman at the photo counter.

She tilted her chin up.

"Hold still."

She held still.

They probably do police mug shots like this, she thought. That lawyer told Morgan that kids with no priors don't do time. Right now, I am a person with no priors.

The license was given to her a moment later. A small plastic rectangle, her picture on the left, vital statistics on the right. She held it by the top and right side, and then by the bottom and left side.

Permission to begin adulthood.

Her license.

Her ticket out of childhood.

She looked at that girl in the photo, and knew, then, who had reached a limit on keeping secrets. She and her teacher went out the door and across the pavement and as they opened their doors, she said quietly, "I took the sign, Mr. Fielding. Just give me tonight to tell my parents."

She knew she had never before looked at Mr. Fielding. Never before seen this person who was half bald, whose tie was old and shiny, whose leather belt was scratched and stretched. And whose shock was complete. He had to steady himself on the car door. Her car door. Her own car, in which she could now chauffeur her brothers and of course kill people if she had a free evening.

Mac came home, dropped his books exactly where his mother told him every day not to, went into his room, and shut the door carefully behind him. The hardware clicked into place. Mac was always gratified by the thickness of his bedroom door.

He lay down on his bed. He didn't turn on the radio, he didn't pick up the phone, he didn't move toward his new comic book or his new Stephen King. He just lay there. Mac loved doing nothing.

He thought about his sister. Mac had expected that little word *reward* to bring Mr. Thompson the information he needed to find Remy.

But nothing had happened.

Remy might slip by. Mom and Dad had little awareness of news. Their own lives seemed to fulfill them enough that they could skip both city and world. Eventually the wrecked car would be towed to a junkyard, people would forget, spring would come, and Remy'd be safe.

She might be safe anyway. Remy did not have the strength to have cut that metal post. Nickie and Morgan therefore had actually committed the crime. She was an accessory. Or maybe just a bystander.

He felt as if he had been lying on the bed all these years for good reason: he knew how to think. Thinking was a valuable skill and people didn't do enough of it.

His sister knocked on the door and came in. They never used to go in each other's rooms. He used to hear rumors about families where the brothers and sisters were friends, but Mac had certainly never given them credence.

Now that she was the bad guy, he liked her. Being rotten and worthless used to be his job. It was nice to pass the torch.

Remy sat on the edge of his bed.

Mac flexed his advice molecules.

"I told Mr. Fielding," said Remy. "He was blaming other people. I think he was getting ready to go to the police. I'll drive to Morgan's, let him know what's happened now, and then come home and tell Mom and Dad."

Mac's brilliant mind emptied. He had no advice. He had no ideas. He could think of nothing helpful. "I'll stay when you tell," he said finally. "Maybe it won't be so bad."

His sister shook her head. "It will be so bad, Mac. It'll be worse."

"What about Nickie?"

She was frightened by that. "What about Nickie?" she said carefully.

"He was there. He's the one who actually chose the sign."

"No," said Remy. "It was just Morgan and me."

"*What?* Why are you lying about *that*?" Mac was incredulous. "Remy, trust me on this one. Let them take the blame. You're just an accessory. You just sat in the car and waited."

"Shut up," said Remy. Her eyes were very bright and slightly crazed. "You are about to have a great privilege. You are my first passenger. I am your legal licensed driver."

* * *

151

Morgan had posed in the middle of Farmington Avenue, legs spread, thumb up, jacket unbuttoned, wallet full.

Two people in her car! He couldn't believe it. Remy'd brought her brother along? Their first drive together, her first solo flight, this girl he was crazy about, and Mac was here?

Okay, he told himself, we're dropping Mac off somewhere. I can live with that.

He wanted to kiss Remy. Feather-light. The way he had in school. Promise of things to come. In front of Mac he'd rather kiss roadkill.

Morgan ran around to the driver's side and tapped on the window till the new driver rolled it down. "Let me see it," Morgan demanded.

She handed over her license.

"Hot off the laminator," he said, grinning, stroking it. "You look great. It's a good photograph, Remy." He stuck his head through the window and kissed her upside down. It was easy to kiss her even with Mac there. She was so pretty. He tumbled around with love, wanting everything perfect for them, wanting the sun always to shine and—

"Look at this!" shouted Morgan. "Rembrandt Marland! I don't believe it! You used your real name!"

"You have to. They make you. You have to bring two forms of ID with your birth date. I had my birth certificate and my baptismal certificate. They both say Rembrandt Valerie Marland."

Morgan laughed. "How'd *Valerie* get in there? I mean, with a first name like Rembrandt, you expect a middle name like Renoir or Monet. Why'd she call you Rembrandt, anyway?"

Remy's laughter turned to tears. "Because she

152

wanted me to be great," Remy said. "She wanted a daughter who was different and great."

Morgan thought she was. And also beautiful and—

"I told Mr. Fielding, Morgan. And now I'm going home to tell my parents what their great and different daughter is really like."

CHAPTER 11

Morgan rarely went into his father's study. Dad would invariably set down his pen, turn away from his computer, drop his newspaper. His father would want to talk, and since Morgan had not talked in years, entering the study had become impossible.

He did not want talk this time either. Or sit.

He didn't want to be in the tall oak chairs with their plump cushions and face that desk with its litter of notes, clippings, files, plans, calendars, and schedules. What would he get from somebody he'd shut out for so long?

Dad doesn't own a gun, so he can't actually shoot the person who took the stop sign. But he might kick me out. Where would I go?

He'd had running-away fantasies. What kid didn't? Vanishing onto a bus or a train; hitchhiking to adventure; living on vending-machine potato chips and smoking the discarded cigarette butts of other travelers.

He didn't want that. He wanted the exact outline of life his parents had drawn up for him: perfection and success. Well, I'm off to a great start, he thought.

His gut hurt, knotting as if he'd gone swimming too far out in water too cold.

He wanted his father to be good and moral and upright, to be just. The kind of person people ache to vote for.

But almost as much, he wanted his father to paint over it; hide what happened to Denise Thompson from Morgan himself as well as from the world.

The collar of Dad's button-down oxford shirt made a little white line above a heavy navy pullover. The knot of his tie hung to the side where he had loosened it. Dad looked up from his work, startled by the sight of Morgan, and instantly looked back down, memorizing where he was, so the interruption wouldn't ruin his work.

Doesn't matter where you are, Dad, I'm about to ruin your work. And your life. But, hey. You have a teenage son, that's the risk you run.

Morgan could not even take a deep breath. His lungs disobeyed him. "Dad?" Even the one syllable snapped in the middle.

His father did not, as in the past, jump up. In that awful silent moment Morgan felt from his father what his father had always felt from him. No interest.

He held himself terribly still. He would not break down; it would be cheating.

You wanted danger, he said to himself, you got it, you worthless whimpering cipher. Denise Thompson didn't want danger. She wanted to live. You took that from her. Admit it, you coward.

"Dad," he said again, and his voice broke.

His father looked shocked, and was out from behind his desk, crossing the room swiftly, wrapping his arms

155

around Morgan. Probably thought Morgan had lost his girlfriend or didn't make the team. The strength under the heavy wool sweater was amazing, as if Dad were the one who did the weight lifting. As if those arms could hold Morgan up out of trouble in which they were both going to drown.

"What is it?" said his father, already in gear to be sympathetic and understanding.

Dad had the right to assume a son of his would never do something that wrong. Other people's kids, but not his. It would mark Mom and Dad as failed parents; people whose children went bad.

"Dad," he said at last, because the only thing worse than telling his father was not telling, "I'm the one who took the stop sign."

Remy had said the words. They were out.

It was her parents who said nothing. They stared at Remy as if she were packaged in a foreign language. Then at each other, their lives no longer comprehensible.

Henry, sensing that good stuff was happening and he wasn't part of it, screamed like police cars going to a hijacking to be let out of his playpen. Mac hoisted him up, setting Henry's fat padded rear on the kitchen counter next to him. Henry immediately wanted the sugar bowl, the paper towels, and the tip of ivy hanging from the planter. You would think in times of crisis that a one-year-old could give it a rest.

"I thought I was a good mother." Mom's voice was as thin and sharp as a razor.

"You are!" cried Remy. "It isn't your fault."

"Good parents don't have children who do things like that."

"It was only a sign," said Mac quickly. "She couldn't know anybody would die. And she didn't actually take it. She was waiting in the car."

"She's sixteen," said Dad. "Why did she think a stop sign was put there? She must at least have suspected that there was a purpose to the sign."

"Oh, God. *God!*" shouted their mother, as if He would come if they raised their voices enough.

"God wasn't there," said Remy.

"What do you mean, he wasn't there?"

"He let Denise Thompson die!" cried Remy.

"Excuse me?" said her mother. The anger in her was ratcheting up. "God did not let Mrs. Thompson die. God doesn't have wrenches and hacksaws. He doesn't supervise dangerous intersections. That's your job. God is a spirit. He brings strength of mind and character."

"He didn't bring me strength of character!"

"He would have if you'd asked."

Remy tried to imagine herself, as they hefted the tools in their hands, looking toward the stars and calling for character. What if I had asked? Would Denise Thompson be alive?

But she had never thought of asking. She had been full of her crush on Morgan, and had thought only of Morgan asking; asking her out.

Her mother was possessed by fury that consumed her body, she was red hot from rage. Her mother advanced on her. Remy felt that her mother had grown claws and a beak, wanted to rip her flesh like a vulture.

"You and Morgan caused Mrs. Thompson to die! Admit it! Admit that you are responsible!"

Her mother's eyes were glittering. Remy backed up into the wall while Henry screamed the screams she wanted to scream. "I do admit it, Mommy," said Remy, sobbing. "That's what I'm doing now. I'm admitting it. I've done a terrible thing."

Her loud, swear-happy father wept. She had never seen him cry. He left the screaming to Mom, as if he himself had broken. "Yes, you have, honey," he said. "If it had been the act of a moment, I could understand it better. I could understand suddenly deciding this would be fun. But this was so planned. It was a strategy, with assignments. You brought tools, you planned cover-ups."

"Remy didn't," said Mac. "Remy was—"

"Excuse me," said their mother. "Remy agreed to go on a sign-stealing expedition. Remy knew she wasn't going over to Lark's to watch movies. It was not a date. A date is something happy and good. They were vandalizing little—"

They all knew the words Mom wanted to use, and were all stunned and sick that such words could apply to Remy.

Mac was her only ally. Remy thought of Mac like God: solid and present and a total surprise. But Mac, like God, solved nothing. He was there, and that was supposed to be enough.

It's not enough, thought Remy. I want to be rescued. I want that night back.

She saw right down her mother's soul, like a doctor looking down a throat, and she saw her mother knowing more than she did. There were no rescues and there was no going back. A woman was dead.

Mom went rigid the way the baby did, arms taut at her side, jaw sprung, teeth clenched. "*How could you do this to me!* I have been a good mother! I have done the right things with you! I have done my best!"

Remy held her hands flat in front of her face, as if she thought her mother would rain blows upon her.

Mac, desperate and furious at everybody, chose to yell at Henry, who was least able to control himself. The family was rioting; they had turned into a mob.

"I know, Mommy," said Remy. "You did do your best. It's me, Mommy. I didn't do my best. I'm sorry."

There was a time of stillness.

A space in which both their hearts raced double time.

Morgan's father drew back from him, to stare into his face. The muscles of his father's jaw and shoulders grew tight and froze into position. Dad's eyes opened a little too wide and stayed there, seeing things he refused to see.

I won't fall apart, Morgan ordered himself. I won't be a little boy. I'm sixteen.

"The stop sign?" breathed his father, pulling farther back. *"Where Denise Thompson was killed? You took that?"*

All the weight lifting in the world did not give Morgan control over his own muscles. He began coming apart, as if tendons no longer connected muscle to bone. It was not the sign that mattered. The sign was nothing. Only Denise Thompson mattered, and she was gone. "Oh, Dad, I killed her!"

The air came out of his father slowly, like a tire going down.

"Dad," said Morgan, unable to swallow, his throat swelling, his fingers thickening.

Slowly, heavily, his father sat down on the wooden visitor chair, and pulled Morgan, all six feet two of him, all hundred and sixty pounds of him, onto his lap. His father's rough cheek pressed against his. He said nothing. Just held his son.

Morgan tried to explain how it had happened.

"Sshhhhhh," said his father.

"I don't want to keep it a secret anymore, Dad. I have to tell."

His father said "Sshhhhhh" again.

"Dad, I can't hide out. I don't want you to hide me. I've tried that, and—it doesn't go away."

"We're not hiding," said his father painfully. "It's just not time for talk yet. Just let me hang on for a while. I've got to let my mind catch up to this." His father brushed possessive hands through Morgan's hair, as if Morgan were a baby. Innocent, and deserving.

After a long time Dad said, "I think you weigh more than I do."

Morgan got up from a lap he had not sat in for a long, long time. Helped his father up. Stood there unable to think clearly about anything, much less his father.

"Tell me everything," said his father. "I love you, Morgan. Just level with me. We'll need it all."

"Who drove?" said Remy's father abruptly.

Remy pressed her lips together.

"Nickie Budie," said Mom. "I looked out the window and saw that little scum and I almost told Remy she couldn't go and then I thought—well, you have to trust them sometime. You have to give them independence eventually. And here we've bought her a car and we're going to trust her with driving her brothers all over the city, so of course I can trust her to . . ." Mom gave Remy a hard, terrible smile.

Dad said, "It was an accident, Jeanie."

Her name was Imogene; he called her Jeanie when he was in love with her. How can Dad be in love with her when she's so angry? thought Mac.

"It was not an accident!" shouted Mom. "You don't spend fifteen minutes with a hacksaw and call that an accident! Is this why you quit the basketball team, Remy? Is this why you didn't want Henry in the pageant? Are you trying to hide out? Blame others? Crawl under a rock? Where you belong?"

"Jeanie, that won't help."

Mom looked at the man who was her husband. "And what will help? Tell me that. What will bring Denise Thompson back?"

Henry chose this time to refuse bed, hate the cookies offered as bribes, and generally outdo himself at being cranky and obnoxious. Along with everything else they had to tolerate the baby, because they couldn't take out their rage on him. The desire to smack Henry became the major desire in the household.

Because that we could do, thought Mac. The one thing we could really do now is shut Henry up. We all want to hit something and he's making the most noise.

Remy went through Kleenex after Kleenex. "I'm sorry, Mommy." She was speaking to their mother, and not their father. Mac wondered if Dad saw, and was hurt by that. Why did Mom's opinion matter more to Remy than Dad's?

Mac saw, confusedly, that he, too, would worry more about Mom's opinion. In some way he had not previously noticed, this was her household, her family, her rules.

"I was worried about the basketball team," said

Dad. He gave a funny little laugh. "I was upset because I'd sort of built my winter plans on going to all the girls' games." He said, "Did you do the mailbox baseball, too, Remy?"

"Dad! I'd never do a thing like that."

"Oh, good, she has standards," said Mom, rage like venom pouring out of her mouth.

"Jeanie, sarcasm won't help either."

Mac wanted Dad not to be scolding Mom. It wasn't helping. Mom's right, he thought. Nothing can help.

"I want not to have done it," Remy said. "I've been trying to think it undone. Praying it unhappened." His pretty sister was unraveling, pulling at her hair and touching her face as if placing Band-Aids on hurts. "But I did do it!" she said, and the sobs burst out in terrible jagged hiccups. "Oh, Mom! I can't bear it."

Mom's anger left as swiftly as it had come, leaving her wilted, like an old flower, ready for discard.

Mac saw how his mother would look in old age.

The last thing that Mac expected was for the Campbells' BMW to arrive in front of the house, and for the two lawyer parents of Morgan to get out, on each side of their son, escorting him up the Marlands' front walk as if into court.

It *is* court, thought Mac. We're going to try Morgan and Remy. If they present a good enough case, we'll stand by them. And if they don't . . . they're on their own.

CHAPTER 12

What a contrast Remy's kitchen was to Morgan's. Nothing sleek, nothing trendy. A harvest-gold refrigerator was taped over with school stuff. A wooden lazy Susan on a fake early-American table was littered with Elvis salt and pepper shakers, a moo-cow coffee creamer, paper napkins falling out of a bent metal holder, a jelly jar filled with colored drinking straws, and a much-chewed pacifier. They all crowded around the table and Morgan had to rest his sweaty hands on yesterday's newspapers, which got newsprint all over them.

Morgan didn't know why they sat in the kitchen. It seemed to him this was a living-room type situation. After a while he realized that Mr. and Mrs. Marland were so shocky, they could not even change rooms. It had happened to them here, and they were stuck here.

He and Remy kept giving the explanations their parents wanted to hear, but the explanations were not, after all, what they wanted to hear.

"Nickie picked the sign," said Remy. "We had the THICKLY SETTLED that Lark needed, and MORGAN ROAD for me, and we didn't need anything more, but Nickie stopped again and . . . well . . ."

163

"And you needed that," said Remy's mother. "Tell me, Remy, in what way you and Morgan needed a stop sign."

Morgan's mother said nothing. Nothing at all. Here was Mrs. Marland exploding with words. Words flung out like daggers, like archery, every word sharp tipped and poison dipped. But Morgan's mother, the lawyer who made a living talking, said nothing.

Dad reached for the big fat gold wall phone, which still had a dial—Morgan hadn't known people had dial phones anymore—and he telephoned Mr. and Mrs. Budie. Morgan's heart and soul hit each other, like the two-person piano piece "Heart and Soul." His guilt-thick fingers slammed against the keys of his fear, playing the same melody over and over.

No! screamed Morgan. You can't talk to Nickie. Don't let them be home. Please, God, no, don't let Nickie talk to Dad.

Morgan was hoping for an accident, that's the kind of person your son is, he enjoyed himself when Denise Thompson bought it, stayed to watch the fun.

He tried looking at Mrs. Marland, but this was a mistake. If Imogene Marland had a microwave big enough, she'd nuke him on high.

He tried looking at Mr. Marland, but Remy's father was rocking the baby, who was almost asleep, but never quite, eyes lifting like a drugged person, more afraid of sleep than life. The sadness on Mr. Marland's face seemed to be for the baby, as if something had happened to Henry and Mr. Marland could not protect him.

As for Remy, he could not quite recognize her. This girl he had known most of his life did not look familiar.

He could not remember kissing that mouth, touching that hair, hearing that voice.

Mr. and Mrs. Budie were home.

His father mostly listened. After a while he disconnected. "Mr. and Mrs. Budie," said Dad in a measured voice, "have explained that their son would never participate in any sort of crime. Would never dream of vandalism. In any event, Nicholas was home that night. They can prove it. They don't know what kind of little liar my son is, but their son, Nicholas, is a fine, upstanding young man."

Nickie's threat was gone. Maybe there was a God. Nickie would hide behind the curtain of his parents and never speak at all.

Morgan didn't even care that the blame was on two now, and not three. That he was the only one now who had chosen the stop sign and cut it off. He would never have to look in his mother's eyes and see that she believed a son of hers could get his kicks that way.

The worst had not happened.

"The question," said Remy's father, "is whether to bring in the police."

Remy had no gods on whom to call. The room was filled with hostile aliens. People who used to be her parents. People who used to be the parents of a friend. They were gritted teeth now, glittering eyes, grating voices.

Her very own father would bring in the police.

"I," said her mother, "am feeling very biblical. An eye for an eye and a tooth for a tooth."

You mean Mr. Thompson ought to be able to kill us back?

Remy, flanked by Morgan's lawyer parents, had the weird thought that she would like to have her own lawyer here right now. She could not speak. She could not argue. Police. Jail. Toilets out in the open and horrible stinking street people and bare mattresses and roaches.

Remy began to sob, and her mother screamed, "How dare you cry? Denise Thompson doesn't get to cry again. She doesn't get to bring up her own baby, and you're the one crying? *Stop crying!*"

Remy stopped crying on the outside, but on the inside she was now screaming. *It was just a sign!* Why can't we all admit that it was just a sign! Everybody does it.

Mr. Fielding arrived just as Mr. Campbell said he was hoping to handle it privately.

The Campbells' BMW shone as if coated with clear nail polish, while Mr. Fielding's old Pontiac had no finish left, and not much color. It was just there, and it had wheels.

Morgan felt his parents' distaste for Mr. Fielding. The man was dressed badly even when dressed well. Every jelly doughnut and coffee with cream lay in rolls around his belly.

Morgan's father commented smoothly on the disturbing fact that Mr. Fielding could not tell Kierstin from Cristin from Lark from Remy. That Mr. Fielding had known all along his class chose sign-stealing for its activity. That as the adult responsible for Driver's Education, Mr. Fielding had neglected both responsibility and education.

Mr. Fielding flinched. "You're right. I was no teacher." He fidgeted with the keys hanging off his belt. "But I didn't cut the sign down. They did. And I think

Remy and Morgan should pay for it somehow. No matter what my problems are and no matter what the legal situation is, the woman is dead."

I respect him, thought Morgan. Dad is basically threatening Mr. Fielding's job, and he's a guy who won't find much else. And still he's hanging in there.

"I haven't called Mr. Thompson yet," said Mr. Fielding, "because when I thought it was Kierstin, Remy had the decency to admit the truth. At least she wasn't going to let somebody be wrongly accused. I give her that much credit. She asked me to wait until she had a chance to talk to her parents. So I did, and now I want to know where we go from here. Because we have to go somewhere."

Mac Marland felt like a video camera. His focus was everywhere, capturing the elusive moments on his mental film.

The two fathers were less angry than the two mothers. The mothers had been personally betrayed; the fathers, momentarily shell-shocked, moved right along.

He knew why, because he was the same.

The fathers were less angry because vandalism, that violent form of showing off, was something they might have done.

Or *had* done.

It was a boy kind of thing. Wherever Morgan Campbell had been, not thinking, not stopping, Morgan's father and Mac's father had been there too.

"Where we go from here?" repeated Mr. Campbell, sounding much too tired to be heading anywhere. "Defacing or removing an official traffic control device is vandalism, a fine of not more than one hundred dollars. Criminal mischief, which is a possible charge, is slightly worse. This covers things like throwing stones at cars or defacing tombstones. A misdemeanor. Fine of no more than two hundred fifty dollars. More serious is malicious mischief. That's a charge usually involving fire alarms, hydrants, railroad crossings, where there's intent to hurt the public. The kids had no intent to hurt. If committed through 'sport' it isn't malicious mischief. All they actually did was steal a sign. Taking signs is almost a suburban hobby. Legally it might even be considered sport."

"So if we go to the police," said Mr. Fielding, "the maximum punishment would be a fine that's only a fraction of your car payment on that BMW."

Mac read a flicker in Mr. Campbell's eyes and knew right away that the Campbells didn't have car payments. They were way out of that league.

"How about negligent homicide?" said Mr. Fielding.

Mr. Campbell shook his head. "The state couldn't really bring a charge, because the kids are removed from the actual cause of death, which was another driver in a truck. Manslaughter has to include a gross deviation from reasonable conduct and an extreme indifference to human life." Mr. Campbell was looking at his son. "Thoughtlessness, which is what happened here, is not manslaughter."

"You mean, nothing will happen to your kids. A woman is dead and nothing will happen."

Mr. Campbell did a strange thing. He rested one hand on Morgan's head and the other on Remy's, like a minister giving a benediction. In the morning, said Morgan's father, he would go see Mr. Thompson. He would find out what it was that Mr. Thompson wanted done.

Mac sucked in his breath. A guy that paid for television time: *Tell me who murdered my wife.* This did not seem like the kind of guy who was going to let it pass.

If I were a parent, thought Mac, I'd do what Nickie Budie's parents did. Slam the door. I'd never do what Mr. Campbell is doing—put my own kid's fingers in the door and then slam it!

For the first time in his life Mac Marland was glad to be a kid. No way would he be the parent knocking on the door of dead Denise Thompson's husband.

"**T**urn onto Warren," said his mother to Dad, who was driving them home. Morgan felt like he was coming down with the flu.

"Nance, I don't want to go to the site of the accident," said Dad.

"Turn onto Warren, Rafe."

Was she going to shove her son out of the car and rub his nose at the base of the stop sign, like a bad puppy who'd messed the floor?

His father turned down Warren. Morgan had a sense that Dad was actually afraid of her; afraid of what she would do; afraid of those words not being said. If Dad was afraid . . .

"And left on Macey," said Mom.

"Nance, please," said Dad.

"*Please?*" repeated his mother. "Is pleasing me part of this equation? My son, does he care about pleasing me? Or pleasing anybody? *He killed somebody.* Where does *please* enter into it?"

Morgan's head brought up the other stuff: how it was only a sign, how he had not actually taken a knife and stabbed Denise Thompson, a collision had killed her, he and Remy were just a contributing factor. But his tongue didn't use the excuses.

169

"Pull in," said Nance.

It was a car dealership. What was she going to do, run him over? It was night, and the lots were bright with theft-prevention lights, but there were no salesmen at this hour. The place was an eerie combination of open and closed.

"Get out," said his mother.

He got out. Dad got out. They were both scared of her.

Rows of shiny parked cars divided into little alleys for his mother to fling herself down, for Morgan to follow, for Dad to bring up the rear. He had the thought that Mom was going to kill him, and he wondered if he should just let it happen. One of the spotlights was failing, and its bulb sang like hornets' nests overhead.

His mother stopped in front of a beautiful cranberry-red Miata convertible. "I bought it for you," she said conversationally. "To celebrate your adulthood. Your new driver's license. You."

It was perfect. Color, accessories, Wow-factor. It was a teenage toy—the best.

"Do you know what I would like to do with it now?" his mother said to him.

He swallowed.

"I would like to take a tire iron and destroy it!" she shouted. "I would like to beat it to death! I could take it out on this car. I could hit it and hit it and hit it until it's dented and ruined and dead! Dead, Morgan! Are you listening to me? Dead! Do you know how long *dead* lasts?"

Dad tried to put his arms around Mom but she was in too deep for arms. "How dare you?" she spat at Morgan. "How dare you take our family, our lovely family, and do this to us? How dare you take Christmas and do this to Christmas?" Her sobs broke, as rough and scraping as the hacksaw on the signpost.

"Oh, Rafe," she said, trying to touch her husband, but stepping back at the same time, "I'm a terrible person. I'm more concerned with being a bad parent in public than with Denise Thompson. She's dead forever, she'll always be dead, and I'm busy being mad about my family."

Rafe Campbell needed to hold each of them, but they were both too far away, and if he stepped toward one, he would step away from the other.

School.

It never faded. Just when you wanted whiteout, there it was, in full color, full time.

Mr. Fielding said, "I canceled the driver's tests for today."

Howls of pain rose from the two kids involved: Lark and Chase. "That isn't fair!" said Chase. "Mr. Fielding, this is life and death! I have plans and—"

"You spoiled brat!" shouted Mr. Fielding. He slammed his fist down on the library table so hard that even outside the glass walls, Mrs. Bee heard and jumped.

Lark said sweetly, "Is this a bad hair day, Mr. Fielding?"

Mr. Fielding stared at her, individually, for the first time in the eight-week session. What he saw so turned his stomach that even Lark dropped her eyes.

"I haven't taught a class yet," said Mr. Fielding. "But I'm going to teach this one. So listen up. You're all brats, one way or another. I don't exempt a single one of you. But I'm worse, because I didn't care. I couldn't

171

have cared less what happened with any of you. I still don't. But there is one thing I care about."

Nobody looked at Mr. Fielding, and nobody looked at anybody else. He was rabid, like a raccoon the sheriff would shoot. The thing was to lie low till it was over.

"She's dead," said Mr. Fielding. "Denise Thompson. She's dead."

That's what this was about? That old wrecked car on the lawn? Several people breathed inner sighs of relief. Several did not.

"You kids are always mentioning life and death," said Mr. Fielding. "Getting into college is life and death. Getting your driver's license is life and death. Having a date is life and death."

He waited so long, they were forced to look up, see what he was doing, see where he was going. When he had them all back, he said, "No. None of the above. Only driving is life and death. Holding a steering wheel is life and death. Choosing to control a car is life and death."

The class relaxed. Yet another safety lecture. Maybe he had just found out that Denise Thompson was really his cousin, or his first wife, or something. It was nothing to do with them.

"I let this class be a joke," said Mr. Fielding. "I let myself be a joke, I let driving be a joke. That's the joke, guys. Because this is the only class you'll ever take where you can go out and kill somebody if you're careless. You fail chemistry or you ace English, it's not life and death. This is the only life-and-death course you have, and I let it be a joke."

People wanted to check the clock or their watches, but they didn't want to move and attract attention.

172

"And those kids? The ones who took the stop sign? Nothing will happen to them," said Mr. Fielding very softly, as if he were speaking to Denise, to her grave, her ghost. "There is no legal remedy. The law can't get at this one."

"I'm a member of SADD," said Christine suddenly. "I think Students Against Drunk Drivers could get involved."

"Only," said Mr. Fielding, "if there were a drunk driver. In this case there's just a couple of stupid teenagers."

"Still," said Christine, "they might have to pay a fine or something."

"So what?" shouted Mr. Fielding. "*So what*? The woman is still dead, do you understand that? Forget fines. Forget SADD. Forget legal anything. She. Is. Still. Dead."

The mall was even Christmasier. At each of the distant four corners of the vast shopping center, school choirs sang carols, and from each door came the canned carols of separate stores. You could not tell one melody from another; it was like a dozen radio stations and a score of wound-up music boxes.

Morgan didn't mind. It kept his head full. He didn't need any space in there in which to think.

"I hate myself," said Remy. "It was a Driver's Ed test, and we both failed. We should have said right there in class that we did it. I mean, Morgan, if we're looking for a punishment to wrap this thing up, we could let the class do it."

They both knew the class would just separate itself, stay silent, and think on other things.

Wrap this thing up, he thought. How on earth do you wrap up death? Morgan wanted to shrug but found he could not make his shoulders do it. It would be shrugging over Mr. Fielding's last hideously separated words. She. Is. Still. Dead.

He finally taught a class, thought Morgan. I hope he knows that. That he was a teacher again. That he mattered. It mattered.

"What are we doing at the mall, anyway?" said Remy.

"We're buying Christmas presents," said Morgan. His laugh sounded shrill to him. "What shall I get for my mother, Rem? She'd really like a tire iron and permission to split my skull open."

"Is she talking to you yet?"

"She's avoiding me. She hasn't been in the same room with me once."

"What do you do about dinner?"

"She doesn't come home. Dad is cooking."

They stared into the window of a seasonal Christmas shop: it had opened in November and would close December 24th. You had to say for Christmas that it was pretty; everything about it was lovely and decorative and sparkly and bright.

"Mom isn't having Christmas," said Morgan. He had not thought he could get those words out. His mother had taken the tree down. Packed up the collection of stars, thrown away the holly. She'd found restaurants in which to hold the rest of the season's parties.

He did not think anything had shocked him as much as the sight of his mother putting away Christmas before Christmas had come.

"How can you not have Christmas?" said Remy. "It comes anyway."

Morgan had found his sister lying on her bed, weeping into her pillow. *There won't be any stockings, Morgan! There won't be any presents! We won't sing any carols and we won't have Christmas dinner. Mom won't even go to the Christmas Eve pageant, because you're doing it, and she says she can't think about how you killed somebody and you get to be in charge of Christmas anyway.*

Starr hated him. His mother hated him. His father was hanging on to everybody's love like double-sided tape.

"Mom says," said Morgan, thinking how friendly and ordinary the word *Mom* was, and how it used to be he couldn't be in the room with her, for no reason, and now she couldn't be in the room with him, for valid reason, "Mom says she can't celebrate hope and joy now."

Remy was looking at crèches. Tiny carved olive-wood camel strings from Israel. A hand-blown crystal manger and baby, as if Jesus were an icicle. A baroque gold and pale blue china Mary from Italy. "I can't decide, Morgan," said Remy, "whether I hate you or I love you."

Morgan marveled that she could say this out loud. Girls could do that, figure out what they were thinking and then use words to tell you. Morgan would have preferred to lift weights the rest of his life than say stuff like that out loud.

Remy was the only person in the world he could really talk to, and yet he wasn't really talking to her; she was talking to him.

Tomorrow would be the talk that counted.

What would he say to Mr. Thompson? I'm sorry? Of course, he could throw in I'm sorry. Like it would matter that he was sorry. Like Denise would be less dead or something.

On Sunday, Mrs. Willit had read from the Book of Job, in spite of the fact that it was the week before Christmas, and she was supposed to concentrate on the coming of baby Jesus. Mrs. Willit had never really caught on to the religious year. Job was from the Old Testament, was thousands more years ago than Jesus, and moreover, was the Bible story most likely to make you detest God, and here she was babbling about Job instead of the Magi or the Star.

Job, pronounced Jobe, was your basic nice guy. So what did God do with the poor slob? Used him as a punching bag. Entertained himself for years by slowly and cruelly destroying the guy's life. It was a bet. God had actually taken a bet that Job would love him anyway.

The Old Testament had a really tough God. He dished it out. You made a mistake, you paid. Even if you *didn't* make a mistake, like Job, you paid.

Mrs. Willit had her usual spazzed-out interpretation. For her, God was this friendly guy who would say, Hey, listen, I know you feel bad about the whole sign thing, so let's call it even. Now get a good night's sleep and don't torment yourself.

Morgan didn't know about God, but the humans in his life certainly didn't plan to call it even.

He'd wanted his father to do the right thing, and he thought maybe Dad was, but what would happen now? If only he could get a sense of what would hit him and Remy.

176

A singing tree-decoration electronically twittered "Silent Night."

He had a sense that he had forever lost "sleep in heavenly peace." Because whether Dad handled things right or not, She. Was. Still. Dead.

CHAPTER 13

"Are you sure this is the right thing to do, Mr. Campbell?" said Remy.

Morgan's father parked the BMW. He took a long time to set it in park and pull on the emergency brake. "No," he said. "I'm not."

Remy had figured a person running for office was always sure of the right thing to do. She felt even sicker than she had during the last twenty-four hours.

The Thompson house was a small ordinary ranch, plain and solid. Its tiny front stoop was the kind where in order to open the door you practically fell into the bushes.

The rain came down. If the temperature dropped a degree or two, it would be snow, and then it would be beautiful and white and pristine; it would be romantic and Christmasy.

But it was only rain.

"Should we have a lawyer with us?" said Morgan.

"I'm a lawyer," Mr. Campbell pointed out.

Remy had thought this was why you had lawyers: so that *they* had to have the meetings.

"You're not a criminal lawyer," Morgan pointed out.

Mr. Campbell looked thinner. His cheek lines were deeper, his voice more tired. "You and Remy are not criminals."

"He thinks we are."

Remy did not ask the God of Tight Situations to help. It would be cheating. Besides, no such god had come through for Denise in her tight situation. Who needed a god who played favorites?

In a split second this door would open. A man would be standing there. She would have to speak. Hi, I'm Remy Marland, how are you, nice to meet you, I'm the one who is partially responsible for your wife's death.

Remy had started saying that to herself. *Partially responsible.* Anything to slide Denise Thompson's death over a space or two.

The door did open.

And Remy didn't care if God played favorites or not. She wanted him around and she wanted him on her team.

Morgan made himself smile at Remy, although he was afraid of being responsible for her; of having to hang on to her as well as himself.

She was composed. She'd worn a skirt, which she didn't often do. Just as Morgan had worn a tie, which he didn't often do.

Dress code for meeting the man whose wife you'd killed.

It'll be over eventually, Morgan told himself. It can't last any longer than your average dentist appointment.

179

Course, it could hurt more. This was, after all, a man who on television and in the newspaper had accused Morgan of being a murderer.

Morgan had looked up Mrs. Marland's quote. Did the Bible actually say you had to repay your crimes "an eye for an eye, and a tooth for a tooth"?

The Bible instruction was a bit more detailed than that. "If any mischief follow, then thou shalt give life for life, eye for eye, tooth for tooth, hand for hand, foot for foot, burning for burning, wound for wound, stripe for stripe."

That was pretty clear.

The first thing Remy thought when she was able to think was *Mr. Thompson is so young. He looks as if he could be in high school with us.*

And the little boy!

How much bigger and sturdier the Thompson child was than Remy's brother. A year made an enormous difference. Henry was a big baby; Bobby Thompson was a little kid.

Bobby was happy to see visitors. "Hi," said Bobby cheerfully. Unlike Henry, whose smile was still partly gums, Bobby had teeth. He waved, although Remy, Morgan, and Mr. Campbell were only a few feet away. "Merry Christmas," added Bobby. In the voice of one giving away a splendid secret, he whispered, "We have stockings."

The Thompsons' tree was short and stocky, ornaments on the bottom branches, eye level for a toddler. There was a fireplace, and two stockings hung from the mantel.

Not three.

* * *

Mr. Thompson was the kind of thin that comes from hyperactivity. Fourth-grade-boy thin. Even his hair was thin. Even his speech. "I've thought of every possible punishment for you two," he said. His thready voice broke and then knit itself back. "I've thought of killing you. I went through a stage of wanting to buy a gun."

I don't want to be here, thought Remy. I don't want to carry any more demons.

"I've thought of prison," said Mr. Thompson. "Prison and walls and cells and bars. You surrounded for twenty years by terrible people who would hurt you."

Mr. Thompson didn't want to look at them any more than they wanted to look at him. The living room received careful scrutiny.

The Thompsons had been too new to housekeeping to have nice furniture. Mismatched cast-offs cluttered the room. Only the windows were newly dressed. Perky starched ivory curtains with cobalt blue bows and a single coordinated lampshade. Cobalt blue and ivory. The color scheme Denise Thompson had been aiming for. But she'd run out of time.

Mr. Thompson's laugh looped around like a strand of yanked-out cassette tape. "I've had crazy ideas too. Like tattooing her name on your arm, so you'd always have to carry Denise with you."

Remy tightened herself against this. It was only a sign. She was not going to carry as much guilt as they wanted her to. He's not tattooing Denise Thompson's name on my arm, thought Remy, and not on my mind or my heart either.

She stole a glance at Morgan, and saw that he, at least, was going to ruin his entire life over a sign. He looked as if Mr. Thompson had already begun stabbing him with needles.

If Morgan still likes me, she thought, which—how could he? But if he still does, I can't let him know what kind of person I really am. Because Morgan is a truly better person. I think he's a Mr. Willit. And I'm a Nickie Budie. Myself first.

All his life Morgan had been taught to say he was sorry.

Sorry for breaking the dish. Sorry for yelling at his sister. Sorry for not mowing the lawn. Sorry for flunking a quiz.

Morgan said, although it was useless, and maybe even insulting, "I'm sorry, Mr. Thompson. I'm sorry she's dead and I'm sorry I can't undo it."

Mr. Thompson grew more taut, and closer to snapping. "I've talked to lawyers. When I realized the police could only charge you with stealing a sign, nothing but a little fine, I thought of bringing a civil suit instead of criminal. I'd lose, but I could muddy your name. At least make it hard for you to go to college in this state. But the lawyers said . . ."

Morgan Campbell was chilled. He did not look left or right; he certainly did not look at his father.

What lawyer had Mr. Thompson spoken to?

The same lawyer Morgan had brought along?

A lawyer with lots and lots of money? A lawyer with lots and lots of experience at changing people's minds?

His father had been here twice, setting this meeting up. The Campbells had money. Clearly the Thompsons did not. Would Dad offer money? Would Mr. Thompson take it? Would a man who had offered a reward on television turn around and accept a reward himself for backing off?

"Tell me what happened," said Mr. Thompson.

Remy appeared to have gone into a coma. Morgan had to do it all. "People were talking about signs," he said carefully. He could not get other kids into trouble with him. That was chicken. It was okay to play chicken, but never okay to be chicken. "Like, a kid who rides his bike wanted BIKE PATH and one of the city kids wanted a country sign. THICKLY SETTLED. It sounded like fun, it didn't sound like a bad thing, and so one night . . . Remy and I went out."

Last night and again this afternoon his father had said, "Morgan, if you've ever listened to me, listen to me now. Tell. The. Truth."

But the truth was, they'd had too much fun to think. Could anybody want to hear that his wife's death was part of a fun time?

"We were having a wonderful time," he said, obeying his lawyer father, and telling the absolute truth. "The first sign we took was THICKLY SETTLED. There was something scary and exciting and even sexy about taking it. Running the risk of getting caught. And the second sign was just a road sign, my name, it was Morgan Road. Remy and I . . . um . . . weren't dating, but we were . . . thinking about it, I guess."

I'm trying to get his sympathy, thought Morgan. Re-create the night so he'll say, Oh well, young love— foolish pranks—not to worry.

"And the road sign was"—he had trouble with this word, but plunged on—"romantic." His throat was dry enough, he was afraid of coughing, and that would be cheating.

"We were flirting," said Remy. He was desperately thankful that she stepped in. "We were in the front seat and giggling and we had our first kiss and even though the word *stealing* went through my mind once, it didn't go through twice, because . . . it was a really neat night."

Remy's doing it too. Building a case that we're really great kids. The stop sign was just a minor slip, let's shrug, okay, because we have our lives ahead of us, and it's too bad that Denise doesn't, but these things happen. No fair pulling any of this burning for burning, stripe for stripe, life for life stuff.

Yet he almost wanted to burn.

"I wanted the Morgan Road sign," said Remy, "because I had a crush on Morgan. Then I thought maybe we'd get ice cream. But somehow we ended up at the corner of Cherry and Warren, and somehow—we took the stop sign." Remy's voice broke and her tears began. Definitely cheating. Begging with weakness. "We didn't mean to hurt anybody. We didn't think taking the sign was . . . well . . . we didn't think."

There. That was it, really. They, honor students, chorus members, churchgoers, didn't think. What made you stop and think, then, if that didn't?

Mr. Thompson's voice was cold as death. "The only reason you kids are here is to put it behind you."

The raging frustration from his television ads came back. He was on his feet, he was glaring into their faces, clenching his fists.

"Do you think I haven't tried to get that night back too?" he shouted. "Do you think I haven't shouted into the void, *Denise! Look twice! Put on the brakes! Go the other way home!*" Mr. Thompson's face was so close to

Morgan's that Morgan breathed in the air Mr. Thompson exhaled.

"You're going to get away with it! Because anything I could do to you I'd go to prison for. And Bobby needs me. So I can't shoot you. I can't stage car accidents for you." He brought his fist down on the arm of his chair, but it was upholstered, and there was no noise, no impact, no result. "Why didn't you tell when you saw the newscast?"

Remy wiped her weeping eyes with both hands. "I was afraid. I'm still afraid. I know that your wife was the most afraid of all, because she's the one who died, and it must have been so scary and painful for her, and I'm sorry."

Baby Henry picked up any emotion in any person at any time, and generally made the Marlands miserable reflecting them back. Bobby, on the other hand, seemed completely insensitive to what was going on. He started a tape in his Fisher-Price cassette player. A husky, recognizable voice sang, "Silly, willy, nilly, old, stuffed with fluff . . ." while Bobby danced and sang along as tonelessly and happily as Winnie the Pooh himself. ". . . Silly, willy, nilly old bear."

Little kids always took to Remy. In spite of the emotion in the room, and three strangers, Bobby got comfortable, and climbed in Remy's lap, wanting to see the funny little silver charms that swung from her necklace.

Remy hugged him, because she could never help hugging little kids. Even when Henry was his most infuriating and wet and sticky, she adored him. And Bobby was so cute.

With clumsy fingers—but so much more adept than

Henry's—Bobby separated the charms and stared wonderingly at each. "A chair!" he said excitedly.

"Three chairs," said Remy, touching each tiny silver seat. "And in between the chairs are music notes. Eighth notes. It's a musical chairs necklace."

Mr. Thompson began to cry. "Denise loved stuff like that." His tears were for a woman he had loved. Remy's tears were for herself. "Bobby's forgetting her. It's so quick. He's perfectly happy with his baby-sitter and his grandmother. In a few months he won't have a single memory of her, and when he's a teenager she'll be nothing but a photograph on the wall."

Mr. Thompson's tears stopped but didn't dry; they lay on his cheeks like tiny creek beds.

Remy took the necklace off to let Bobby play with it. He set it on the coffee table to see if the charm chairs would stand, and they did. He crowed happily.

"I want you to pay," said Mr. Thompson drearily. "But what's going to happen is, you will forget. You have to forget, in order to survive. Bobby will forget. My sister thinks I'll remarry. And Denise will evaporate."

Bobby climbed onto his lap so daddy would admire the neat necklace. Mr. Thompson brushed his son's hand away. "This is a two-holiday murder," he said. "A Thanksgiving and a Christmas death. Every Thanksgiving dinner and every Christmas morning as long you live, I want you to remember Denise. Who doesn't have holidays now. I want your Christmases ruined."

Mr. Thompson peeled the necklace out of Bobby's fingers, and Bobby wailed and fought for it.

"He can keep it," said Remy quickly.

Mr. Thompson looked at her incredulously. "I think we have enough souvenirs of what you did to us."

Outside the rain was still falling.

The same monotonous heavy rate as before.

Puddles filled low spots in the yard.

Mr. Campbell got in the driver's seat and turned on the engine and the wipers. The wipers clicked arhythmically, the left one earlier than the right.

In the comfortable warm backseat of the BMW, Morgan took Remy's hand. "Dad?" he said.

"Yes?"

"Can you still run for office?"

"Yes," said his father. Without excitement. Without enthusiasm. His fuel, like Mr. Thompson's, was used up. Nobody got into office without tremendous energy. If Morgan had consumed his father's energy, the campaign was doomed.

"This isn't a skeleton in your closet?" Morgan asked.

"No, it isn't, Morgan," said his father quietly. "It's a skeleton in *your* closet."

CHAPTER 14

Remy rested her fingertips on the chair seats of her necklace, as Bobby had. I'll always wear it. It'll be Denise Thompson for me. She'll be my musical chairs. Maybe she'll make me a better person. Or at least a thinking person.

What a simpleminded idea. Jewelry improves the soul. Right.

Remy yearned to be in her own bedroom, door tightly closed. Flat on the mattress, staring up at the ceiling, letting the nightmare drip out of her, like a reverse intravenous.

Her mother obstructed the path to the stairs. Her mother seemed immense, impassable, like a falling-rock zone in the mountains. My mother doesn't like me, thought Remy. It was worse than knowing that Denise Thompson was dead.

Remy clung to the necklace. What if life itself was musical chairs? Nothing but chance?

Mom demanded that Remy repeat every word of the visit to Mr. Thompson.

Mac listened silently. Dad stayed in the TV room with the baby. Remy had hardly seen her father since the night she'd told her parents. Mom was taking her solace in screaming at Remy. Dad was burying himself in television.

"Do you need me to help with dinner," said Remy carefully, "or may I go to my room?"

"And what do you plan to do in your room? Decide which wall to decorate with stop signs?"

Remy no longer had any temper. There was no anger in her, no rebellion, no lashing back. She wondered if this would last the rest of her life, or if she would recur, like a cosmic event, and explode. "I need to empty my mind."

"Empty your mind?" repeated Remy's mother. "Excuse me, Remy." Her mother said that a lot now.

Oh, Mom, please excuse me, thought Remy.

She wanted to shake her mother, demand love, demand to be excused.

But then where would the punishment be?

"The drivers today," said Mr. Fielding, "will be Remy and Morgan."

His voice was hard. He had named one too few student drivers.

"Woooo-ee!" said Lark. "And what did you two get up to in the backseat?"

The class laughed and made backseat sex jokes.

Mr. Fielding gestured for Remy and Morgan to go first, making it the only time that his students had walked ahead of him to the car.

Our execution, thought Remy. He's going to take us to the stop sign and get rid of us.

The strange lack of anger that had possessed her for so many days was still there. She cooperated fully. It was as if she yearned for punishment. Did little mice and rabbits yearn for the owl to swoop down? Surely all creatures fought to live, not to surrender.

Mr. Fielding drove, and they went in his car, not the student driver car. Remy and Morgan neither looked at nor touched each other, but merged in a strange vibrating fear. They had no idea what Mr. Fielding meant to do.

A cemetery stretched for many acres on the edge of the old part of town. It was the sort of cemetery where you could have any kind of stone you wanted, so there were cenotaphs and obelisks, curling angel wings and glistening marble slabs like steps to the Pentagon. Many tired flags stood on pencil thin sticks to mark the graves of veterans, and, horribly, bronze baby shoes marked the graves of children.

Mr. Fielding drove on narrow gravel paths at five miles an hour. "Is this a lesson in death?" said Morgan.

"I'm looking for Denise Thompson's grave."

Mr. Fielding parked. They got out of the car and walked between a dozen grassless graves. Even the ground was dead. They talked in whispers, as if the dead were listening in.

Nestled against Denise Thompson's stone were bouquets of real flowers, frozen black. Dead like Denise. Her name and her dates were chiseled into the stone.

Remy tried to be a ball of nothingness, a mitten in a pocket, a plastic flower. When Mr. Fielding jammed his hands into his pants pockets, she almost expected him to pull out a gun and kill them both.

"It was my fault," he said. "It's always the fault of the grown-up in charge, and so it's my fault. I want you to know that."

Morgan said irritably, "There was no grown-up in

190

charge, Mr. Fielding. We were on our own and we were stupid, and it isn't your fault."

At last they touched, Morgan first, his arm wrapping her waist, pulling her in against his side. She could barely feel the real Morgan through the thickness of her puffy jacket.

Their teacher regarded them sadly. "I'm trying to make it easier for you."

"But why?" said Remy confusedly. "You're the one who came over and said we had to pay."

"I don't know why. I don't know anything about this. I'm trying to spread the blame, I guess."

"It isn't peanut butter," said Morgan. "Blame doesn't spread."

They stood for a long time, like some terrible poem they made you study in school. Eternal staring at sentences about death. We'll be here for days, thought Remy, but when we get in the car and I look at the dashboard clock, it'll have been only five minutes. Kind of like Mrs. Willit's sermons.

Mr. Fielding went back to the car, and Morgan and Remy followed.

Mr. Fielding turned the key too long, grinding the gears hideously.

Morgan said, "Thank you."

For a minute Remy could not figure that one. Thank you?

For letting go, she realized. My mother won't let it go, my father won't start, Morgan's mother won't let it go, his father is doing his duty.

But Mr. Fielding is letting it go.

She tried to think who was the responsible adult here, and who knew how to teach, but still, like chance and death, none of it made sense.

* * *

On the afternoon of December twenty-fourth Morgan showed up. Mrs. Marland was not polite.

"May we please talk for a minute?" said Morgan. "The Van Holland baby has an earache. We need Henry to be Jesus after all."

Her mother's voice was as ugly and rusty as abandoned garden tools. "Use an empty manger."

"Empty?" repeated Morgan.

"I think it would be very symbolic."

"But isn't the point . . . that Jesus . . . um . . ." Morgan could not seem to remember the point.

"That Jesus is always there," said Mac, the least likely person in America to have paid attention to Sunday school lessons. "Love is always there."

"Remy and Morgan are proof that it's all emptiness," said Mrs. Marland. "I was stupid. I actually believed that good things would happen if you did your best." She looked at her daughter. "That good parents would have good children."

Henry came in, dragging his blanket. He had the dazed grogginess of a child napping with his eyes open. Is that my life from now on? thought Remy. Dragging from room to room and never waking up from this nightmare?

"Mom," she said finally, "you do have good children." She was not crying. Perhaps her need had gone beyond tears into the dry desert of not being loved. "I was very dumb for ten minutes, Mom, and being smart about it now doesn't change it. I don't excuse what Morgan and I did. I know Denise Thompson is still dead. But you're still my mother."

Her mother didn't even bother to look at her.

Remy was desperate for love, so she lifted her little

brother up on her shoulder. His four-toothed grin completely filled his face. He had his sister and he was high enough to look around. What else was there? Henry spread soppy kisses on his sister's face, resting his hot little open mouth against her cheek.

Her mother tried to leave the room. Remy blocked her. "Mom, you've spent our entire lives telling us that love is the only thing that matters. Now when love really does matter, *and I really do need you,* you're not trying."

"I'm too mad at you to try!"

"I know that. I don't care how mad you are at me. I'm very mad at me too. But you have to go on loving me."

"I don't feel like it," snapped her mother, sounding like a two-year-old herself.

Touch me, Mom, prayed Remy. Please get close to me!

But her mother did neither.

And it was Mac who finally lost his temper. "What about me?" he yelled. At Mom, not at the ones who had done wrong, but Mom. "You think this is relaxing to live with? You and Dad, behaving like this? What does it mean, anyway? I do any little thing wrong in my entire life, and my mother and father will check out of the line? Write me off?"

His mother's voice was ice. "It isn't any little thing, Mac. She. Is. Still. Dead."

"Oh, God," whispered Morgan.

They had nearly forgotten Morgan. Now he reappeared in their sight, oddly thin and worn. Remy wondered about God: if he was really there, really about to answer or to worry.

Mrs. Marland put her arms around Remy, around

Morgan, and around Mac, with Henry in the middle spurting up like whipped cream from a can. "I love you all, I do, I love you so much, but I can't seem to get past being *so mad at you!*"

She was out of breath, as if the grand embrace in which she held a stranger's son, and a stranger daughter, had been a marathon. "Nothing has ever happened to us before that your father and I couldn't make better," she said. "I can't believe the first real test is death. Because nobody can make that better."

But she had made it better. So much better.

No matter how angry Mom was, and maybe would always be, Remy was partly excused.

I know, Mr. Thompson, she said to him in her heart, that being excused isn't part of the deal. But my mother has to go on loving me. Denise would go on loving Bobby.

Her eyes filled with tears, and through the blur she saw that the one who was healed the most was Mac; she had not even known that Mac was damaged; she had been too self-absorbed to read his fears.

Mac, her holy-terror brother, was the one who most needed his family in love with each other.

Five weeks, start to finish, sign to sign.

Morgan was dazed by the swiftness of it.

Only the pageant was slow. Camels plodded, sheep stumbled, and the kings drew nigh.

Henry took one look at those crawling, baaing first graders in sheep costumes and refused to go near the manger. So Morgan decreed two Marys: the original cast member to wear the blue gown, and Remy to keep Jesus from breaking his way out of the stable.

"Bunch of perverts in this church," Taft whispered

to Morgan. "Joseph has two wives, one king's a girl, and Queen Joanne the Normal's in charge."

Morgan smiled in the dark and drifted away. He was many things right now, but normal wasn't one.

"I want you and Remy to go back to normal," his father had said last night.

Nobody else here is going to achieve this pinnacle of success. Normalcy. Think about it, Morgan. Thank your lucky stars.

Morgan tried to believe he had a lucky star, he who had killed by accident. That was the thing, his father said: to remember that Denise Thompson's death had been an accident. That it was only a sign.

And Mr. Thompson backing off? Had that been an accident? Or had Dad, so to speak, fixed the fight?

Did Morgan want to know?

"We'll always go to church now," Starr had said grumpily. "You go and kill people, Morgan, there's no way out. Even when Dad wins, we'll have to keep going to church."

But he was not sure Dad would run. He had taken the stuffing out of his father, and nobody ever ran for office without it.

"Was it moral," he'd asked his father, "for Remy and me to get off?"

"Stop talking and get dressed," his mother had said. "No matter what the moral situation is, nobody goes to the Christmas Eve service in sweats." She would not look at her son. Only at his clothes.

When they were leaving for church, Starr asked the question Morgan could not. "Mom, do you still love Morgan?"

Morgan held himself against the answer.

She hadn't looked at him. She'd looked at her black

195

gloves and her Christmas-bells coat pin. Shrugged. "I'm working on it."

"I still love you, Mom," he had said hesitantly.

"Apparently not enough to behave the way I taught you."

He wanted to tell her what he had just learned at the Marlands': that you can be very very mad and still love your kid. But he couldn't talk to his mother the way Mac and Remy talked to theirs.

Starr was the third king, the final figure to come down the aisle. She had gotten the red robe after all. It spread behind her, velvet encrusted with glittering gems.

Morgan sighed and sent the final king down the aisle.

There was no moral to the story. It could have been any global conflict they studied in Current Events. A nightmare that began, killed, and ended. And now what? Was anybody better for it?

Starr reached the stable.

Mrs. Willit read at the rate of one syllable per motion. Morgan was sliding into a coma. It's my pageant, he thought, and I'm so bored, I think it's already February.

"The kings . . . knelt . . . down . . ."

(Starr hadn't cared for this. "I'm a king," she said irritably, "I don't kneel." "That's the *point*," said Kyle. "They kneel for *Him*.")

". . . and worshiped," said Mrs. Willit.

(Starr didn't want her crown tipping off when she bent her head and had informed the director of the pageant that she, personally, was not bowing, and the director informed his sister that he, personally, would just remove her head instead. "Oh," said Starr.)

"And Mary remembered these things," said Mrs. Willit, "and pondered them in her heart."

In the soft light of the candles Morgan saw tears on more than one face. Did everybody have a Denise Thompson to ponder?

The pageant ended.

Candles were blown out gently, shielded by cupped hands. The lights went back on. Sheep and shepherds turned back into kids, hurling costumes on the floor, dropping crook and staff, running to the bathroom before it was too late, demanding something to eat.

"Good pageant," Morgan's mother managed, and turned away, quickly leaving the church to wait in the car rather than be next to Morgan.

He wondered if he would ever be a good son again in her eyes, or just a person who completed tasks.

On the far side of the church Taft waved the royal wave. Remy and Morgan waved back.

She wanted to throw herself on Morgan, take him home with her. But it was his mother's love Morgan wanted, and his eyes followed Mrs. Campbell longingly.

"Merry Christmas," said Remy softly, and their eyes met. Morgan held her, lightly. Not a hug full of anger and love and forgiveness like Mom's. But a closeness that went all the way through. "Well, maybe not merry," said Remy. "But Christmas."

Morgan smiled. Oh, she loved his smile! "Christmas," he agreed.

The church was full: light that sparkled gold and silver; music from the organ; scent from the pine boughs; neighborly love from families and friends.

Mr. Thompson's punishment: May every Thanksgiving and Christmas be ruined.

She saw that you could not ruin Christmas. Christmas stayed beautiful even when you were not.

But, oh! how you could ruin a life.

Remy marveled that anything was still a risk, but it was. Remy was still afraid of things, including admitting to Morgan how deeply she loved him. His suffering was intense. Almost chosen: as if he had willed Mr. Thompson to give him something heavy to carry.

Remy's parents collected her. Henry was asleep on Dad's chest.

"Let's head home," said Remy's father. "We still have presents to wrap."

Morgan seemed to want to say something, but couldn't get it past his lips. He half shrugged and half smiled. Morgan was very close to the edge. Remy did not want to put him over. But a wave good-bye wasn't enough, not when she wasn't sure if he'd get through the twenty-fifth. She hugged him, and the strength of his hug back was a Christmas present. "It's a wrap," said Morgan softly, and she knew what he meant: it was over, it was wrapped, it was done.

Mac followed Mrs. Campbell out of the church.

At the same time that Mac agreed with Mr. Thompson—Christmas should be destroyed in memory of the destruction of Denise—he completely disagreed. Mac had never thought about family, much less how much family mattered. Now he felt he was the only one who really understood.

You could be wrong, but you must be loved.

He wanted Morgan to have Christmas.

"Hi, Mrs. Campbell," he said.

"Merry Christmas, Mac," she said with an effort.

"It'll only be merry," he said to her, "if you go back inside."

She stared at him, name-calling with her expression: You runty interfering little twerp!

"You're his mother," said Mac.

"And my son was a—"

"Jerk," said Mac. "But you aren't. You're his mother. He needs you."

I'm the shepherd, thought Mac.

It was the only Christmas present Morgan could give Remy: pretending it was a wrap.

He tilted his head back to control a rush of tears. It was just a sign, he thought. I've got to hold on to that, whether my mother can or not.

Volunteers made cleanup quick. In moments only the wreath on the door and the poinsettias on the window ledges remained. The church was completely empty, and yet it seemed to stay full, as if hope and love were still around. "I don't think I deserve love," said Morgan.

"No," said Dad softly, "you don't deserve love."

Morgan's heart lurched. He did not know how he could manage to get down the church steps and over to the car, never mind the rest of his life. Even Dad was against him now?

"That's the thing about love," said his father, wrapping a Christmas arm around his son. "Nobody deserves it. Love just is."

The arm holding Morgan up turned him toward the arched wooden door, hung with holly.

His mother was coming back for him.

Hope and love were still around.

A Selected List of Fiction from Mammoth

While every effort is made to keep prices low, it is sometimes necessary to increase prices at short notice. Mandarin Paperbacks reserves the right to show new retail prices on covers which may differ from those previously advertised in the text or elsewhere.

The prices shown below were correct at the time of going to press.

☐ 7497 0847 6	**The Face on the Milk Carton**	Caroline B Cooney	£3.99
☐ 7497 0343 1	**The Stone Menagerie**	Anne Fine	£3.99
☐ 7497 2304 1	**Shadow Man**	Cynthia D Grant	£3.99
☐ 7497 2651 2	**Creepers**	Keith Gray	£3.99
☐ 7497 2641 5	**Heart to Heart**	Miriam Hodgson (editor)	£3.99
☐ 7497 1793 9	**Ten Hours To Live**	Pete Johnson	£4.50
☐ 7497 0281 8	**The Homeward Bounders**	Diana Wynne Jones	£4.50
☐ 7497 1707 6	**Who'll Catch the Nightmares?**	Linda Kempton	£3.99
☐ 7497 1061 6	**A Little Love Song**	Michelle Magorian	£4.99
☐ 7497 1482 4	**Writing in Martian**	Andrew Matthews	£2.99
☐ 7497 0323 7	**Silver**	Norma Fox Mazer	£3.99
☐ 7497 1699 1	**You Just Don't Listen!**	Sam McBratney	£3.50
☐ 7497 1685 1	**The Boy in the Bubble**	Ian Strachan	£3.99
☐ 7497 0009 2	**Secret Diary of Adrian Mole**	Sue Townsend	£4.50
☐ 7497 0333 4	**Plague 99**	Jean Ure	£3.99
☐ 7497 2617 2	**Secrets**	Sue Welford	£3.99
☐ 7497 0147 1	**A Walk on the Wild Side**	Robert Westall	£3.50

All these books are available at your bookshop or newsagent, or can be ordered direct from the address below. Just tick the titles you want and fill in the form below.

Cash Sales Department, PO Box 5, Rushden, Northants NN10 6YX.
Fax: 01933 414047 : Phone: 01933 414000.

Please send cheque, payable to 'Reed Book Services Ltd.', or postal order for purchase price quoted and allow the following for postage and packing:

£1.00 for the first book, 50p for the second; **FREE POSTAGE AND PACKING FOR THREE BOOKS OR MORE PER ORDER.**

NAME (Block letters)..

ADDRESS..

....

☐ I enclose my remittance for..........................

☐ I wish to pay by Access/Visa Card Number

Expiry Date

Signature ....

Please quote our reference: MAND

Also by Caroline B Cooney

THE FACE ON THE MILK CARTON

The little girl on the milk carton stared back at Janie . . . an ordinary little girl, a three-year-old who had been kidnapped twelve years ago from a shopping mall in New Jersey. "It's me," whispered Janie. "But I have a mother and father . . . I have a childhood . . . I was not kidnapped . . . kidnapping means bad people . . . I don't know any bad people . . . therefore I am making this up . . . "

Fifteen-year-old Janie can't believe that her loving parents had kidnapped her, unitl she begins to piece together things that don't make sense. Why are there no pictures of Janie before she was four? Why is the dress in the photo in her house?

Something is terribly wrong and Janie is almost too afraid to find the truth.

Janie's story continues in *Whatever Happened to Janie?* and is concluded in *The Voice on the Radio*.